M.M

The Shed

Kit&Kel Press 🐓

The Shed

First Edition 2003

Published by Kit&Kel Press
Warwickshire UK

Proof editing by Sarah Burch
Illustrations, design and typeset by Kit Harris
Printed in the UK

Distributed by Transglobal Emporium
PO Box 116 Cambridge CB4 2EA UK

www.transglobal-emporium.com

ISBN 0-9546514-0-5

The Shed

By M.M.

Illustrated by Kit Harris

Kit&Kel Press

To the Shed Folk

All sleeping sound in their suburban beds
Amidst the sentinel ranks of English sheds

~

Now if the harvest is over
And the world turned cold
Give me the bonus of laughter
As I lose hold

Sir John Betjeman (1906 - 1984)

~

And where there were sheds things were bound to rot

Stella Gibbons, *Cold Comfort Farm* (1932)

CHAPTER ONE

Winter

The frozen earth crunched beneath his new size twelve rubber boots. The tall, gaunt, bearded figure bounded swiftly along the allotment path, the woolly ears of his tracker hat flapping up and down, his hands so firmly jammed into his trouser pockets, that his elbows were locked straight. Thomas De'Ath combined his long, forward-stooping gait with a gaze through thick spectacle lenses towards the horizon, giving the impression of a loping, myopic giraffe.

There were few gardeners on Oldside Allotment that Boxing Day morning. An old man pitched a brand new fork into a compost heap, the prongs flashing bright in the low sun, releasing steam into the crisp air. "A Christmas present," thought De'Ath, "perhaps from a son or a daughter."

He pictured the old man reading the label, tearing at shiny paper, and beaming with as much surprise and satisfaction as his grandsons had before it was light. De'Ath had retained through his sixty years the delight of receiving Christmas presents. The day before, as he had unwrapped the gardening boots his wife had bought for him, he had laughed in delight. Like a boy with new football boots, he could hardly wait for Boxing Day to try them out.

De'Ath had seen the old man on the allotment regularly, but had never yet spoken to him. He did not know his name, but Christmas seemed the appropriate time to break the ice. "Merry Christmas, forker!" he called to the old man, who froze, mid-lift. He looked over at De'Ath, pitching his fork into the ground. He screwed up his eyes.

"What did you just call me?" He was used to receiving verbal abuse from the youth of Oldside, but rarely from his fellow gardeners.

"Erm, forker. Sorry, I don't know your name, and, well, you were forking."

The old man, small and wiry, pulled his fork from the earth and moved towards De'Ath suspiciously. He stopped and looked him up and down. "Odd fish, this bloke," he thought. "Are you trying to be funny?" he demanded.

De'Ath was almost never trying to be funny. "No, not at all. I am Tom De'Ath." He held out his gloved mitt stiffly. The ancient gardener eyed him warily. "This joker will just as likely pull me over in the muck," he thought.

"Those new boots?" asked Philp.

"Yes, for Christmas," replied De'Ath, his hand still extended. "From my wife."

"Steel toe-caps I hope?"
"Not exactly." De'Ath retracted his arm at last. "Le

Chameau Bridge Boot, made from natural rubber with leather insole. Easy to put on thanks to its two elastic gores at the sides, which provide superior foot support. Rather a fine shade of midnight blue, wouldn't you say?"

Philp peered at De'Ath's feet. "Look like they'd be better worn at a disco, Mr. Death. Now what if some fool was to do this…"

Philp raised up his fork, and slammed the prongs into the toecap of his own right boot. The boot was as tough as flint, the prongs rang like tuning forks in the cold air as they bounced upwards. He took a mock-menacing step towards De'Ath, who regretted that he should have tried to greet this clearly dangerous senile, and he began to move away sideways, in a crab-like movement down the path. "Well, Merry Christmas, Mr. er,…?" he called, mid-scuttle.

"Philp. Philp the Forker, eh?" replied the now toothless-grinning, ancient gardener, brandishing the fork towards the retreating De'Ath.

"Another insane lunatic unleashed by Care in the Community. Have to watch out for him," thought De'Ath, as he loped on. Further up the track, he inspected a garden shed of orange cedar panels and neatly pinned asphalt roof. With a bony index finger protruding from his fingerless mitten, he cleared a saucer-sized circle from the frosted windowpane and peered into the shed's interior. Not a single object was to be observed within.

Ramming his hands back into their accustomed pockets, De'Ath turned and bounded on. Forty yards away was another shed, but of an altogether different composition from the cedar box he was leaving behind in the slight morning mist. The larger part of this edifice was the curving corrugation of an Anderson bomb shelter. Spliced to this was a wooden hut of extreme antiquity, consisting of old posts, assorted wooden planks, and a mosaic roof of corrugated iron patches. The door, its green paint peeling and crookedly hung on rusting hinges, was evidently a discard from a public house toilet. A grimy yellowing perspex sign read "Gents". The windowpane, coated with green film, had long ceased to be translucent. A rusty, cockeyed weather vane was jammed into the fractured guttering and, being unable to revolve, indicated a permanent northerly wind.

Twenty paces from the Shed, De'Ath noticed a curl of smoke escape between roof and eaves, and at five paces, the smell of pipe tobacco reached his nostrils. Pulling the rickety ceramic handle of the door, the whine of the hinges accompanied the sound of a whistling kettle. The steam hit his chilled spectacle lenses, and De'Ath was blinded as he entered the comforting warmth.

"Eeeh, that were gut timin' Tommyboy, kettles just come t'boil! Put wood in th'ole, man, yer letting all th'eat art! Think of me ath-ritis, lad!"

A thickset man was hunched over, busy with metal camping mugs, PG tips tea bags, and a flask of milk. The first thing to notice about Ron Bullock was his neck. Like that of a tortoise, it was able to elongate to jut the square Yorkshire miner's chin, or to retract into many belligerent ruddy folds, which fell around his throat. His head was

bald, his face was scarlet and chubby, full of honesty and absent of wisdom. As he offered a steaming mug to his friend, he pulled vigorously from a pipe carved into the shape of a bull's head.

"Great new pipe, Ronald," exhaled De'Ath, cleaning his glasses of condensation and settling into the battered, punctured splendour of an old wingback leather armchair. "Looks like a hand-carved meerschaum to me."

Bullock settled into an identical chair, also sighing loudly as he became seated. "Aaaaah. Oh, do you like it, lad? Sheffield bull, it is. And yer right, cut out of the Turkish stone. From me sister, for Christmas. Come on, knock yer own out, I've got some gut stuff here."

De'Ath set about knocking out and cleaning a wooden pipe, which he had taken from a rack on one of the many shelves.

"Now I cannot understand you sticking with the briar. The stone pipe is the one, Thomas. Beyond doubt." Bullock sat back in his chair, a contented smile on his lips as he inhaled, as if to affirm his assertion.

"Oh, I'll always be a briar man," replied De'Ath quietly. "Just think of those gnarly old roots of the white heath tree, clinging onto the Mediterranean crags. Carved into a perfect bowl. This is a Don Carlos SL1 Bent Billiard. One of the finest pipes ever made."

"Each to thee own, then. Now, I hope you like this." Bullock removed a plaid pouch from his brown moleskin waistcoat pocket and handed it to his friend. "I believe we can agree:

when it comes to tobacco, English is superior to Aromatic or Burly!"

"Oh, now, that we have in common, Ron. Now, what have you got here, it smells fantastic. The dark Navy Flake perhaps?"

"Nope, guess again." Bullock's small blue eyes narrowed and twinkled.

"Could it be the Red Cake?" enquired De'Ath, after a lengthy pause for thought.

"Getting warmer, lad, it's a Virginia, but I won't keep y'in suspenders... it's the St James Flake!"

"Ah, the St. James, I've got it now, yes, of course, that 'mushroomy' flavour!"

The two men sat in contented silence, breathing large clouds of smoke into the recesses of the Shed and gulping tea. At each gulp, there was a loud "Aaaaah" from Bullock. "I must say, they don't make a bad cuppa these tea bags these days, eh? Must be those ten thousand tiny perforations. Bella will never use 'em. "Sweepings up," she says. Likes her pot does Bella. But how on earth you can make a tea bag last three mugs is beyond me though, Tom."

De'Ath preferred his tea quite weak, and had the habit, found annoying by many, of retaining a used tea bag not once, but twice.

"Oh, my Dot's the same!" replied De'Ath, "always a pot

with loose PG. We liked the monkeys you know."

"Oh, aye," chuckled Bullock, "t'monkeys eh? Coo-eee Mister Shifter! Can yer ride tandem?"

De'Ath smiled wistfully over the rim of his camping mug. "1956 they started. Oh, they used to make us laugh. 'Daaa-aad, do you know the piano's on my foot?'" he said in a stupid voice. Bullock continued his chuckling. "By 'eck, 1956, that must have been one of the first ads on, eh?"

De'Ath thought for a few moments, nodding whilst he pulled on his briar pipe. "The first advertisement shown on British TV was for...SR Toothpaste, screened at...9.01pm on...September 22nd, 1955," he announced slowly.

Bullock nodded sagely. He had lately become used to De'Ath's prodigious memory for trivia. It would have made him an excellent man to have in a quiz team, but he was much too slow with the answers.

"I can't believe they are replacing them with those bloomin' Wallis and Grommit animations," continued De'Ath.

"Oh, they're not are they?" responded Bullock, quite crestfallen. "Oh, they'll ''ave to 'ave 'em back. I mean, since they took the Tetley Tea Folk off, the sales have plummeted. Fourteen percent, tha' knows."

"Heh, what next, they'll be taking Tony the Tiger off Frosties," chuckled De'Ath, but Bullock leaned forward, suddenly fierce. The neck jutted, the eyes bulged, the lower lip protruded, the pipe-tip pointed, freezing the half smile on De'Ath's face.

"Oh, they wouldn't do that, Tom," he said quietly and resolutely. "I love that tiger." Bullock continued to stare intently at De'Ath after he had said his piece, as if De'Ath himself was the architect of the heinous plot to remove the beloved tiger. This made De'Ath rather uncomfortable. He averted his eyes from the Yorkshireman's gaze, who did look slightly deranged.

"No, I'm sure they won't, then," muttered De'Ath, picking up his tea mug and sipping the cold dregs nervously. "I'm sure they won't."

"No, they won't."

Bullock sat back in his chair, his arms folded. He had settled that business.

It was quiet for a while. De'Ath was thinking about which of the monkey adverts he liked the best. Bullock was thinking of whether he preferred PG or Tetley's tea.

"They are like little pyramids, these, aren't they?" said De'Ath suddenly, picking up the tea bag from the grimy plastic tray on the floor of the Shed. "Maybe I could get four out of these."

"Tom, do you realise how much these bags cost us? Less than 2p each. I mean, they don't even do ha'pennies any more! I admire your thrift, like, but tha' musn't scrimp on good things in life like a nice tea bag."

"I used to love the old ha'pennies, with a clipper on the tail. Shove ha'pennies. That was a game, eh, Ron?"

"Oh, aye. Cracking game. They used to have a board, tha'knows in t'Grasshopper, with polished ha'pennies. Oh, aye, cracking game. Unlike bar billiards. Wretched game that. And you know my favourite pre-decimal coinage, Tom?"

"Go on."

"The duodecahedral…"

"…threepenny bit.

"Correct."

"Have a guess when the first tea bag was produced, Ron. I'll bet you'd be surprised."

"Hmm, let me 'ave a think. Sixties invention, I reckon. A bit of Harold Wilson's white hot technology. 1965."

"Wrong."

"1969."

"Wrong. 1904. New York tea and coffee shop merchant, Thomas Sullivan, sent samples of his various tea blends to customers in small hand-sewn muslin bags."

"Bugger. 1904. An American invention. Fancy that. I'd have sworn that were a British invention, that! Y'now, I were just thinking, just now, what was me favourite tea."

"PG and the monkeys for me."

"Aye, I know it ought to be Tetleys fo' me, but I'd have to admit its PG for me an' all. Y'know, lad, it seems odd, here we are, connoisseurs of the pipe weed, yet our favourite brew is PG Tips. D'you not find that odd?"

"Nothing wrong with PG, Ron. Do you know what it stands for, by the way, PG?"

Bullock considered this carefully. "I don't believe that I do. Is it after a region in India, or summat?"

"No," replied De'Ath firmly, leaning forward. "It stems from when tea was a medicinal brew. PG is 'pre-gestive', or before-meal. And 'Typhoo' is Chinese for doctor."

"Well I never. You are the proverbial fountain of knowledge, Thomas, you really are. By the way, what is the proverbial fountain of knowledge? There's a gut question for thee to muse upon."

Musing was what De'Ath liked to do best. He would go into a musing trance, with the aid of a good pipe tobacco. Bullock was fascinated by this, and by De'Ath's bookworm knowledge, and was very happy to sit and think his own, less exacting thoughts, as the muser did muse.

Around them in surreal chaos lay an astonishing variety of gardening tools fashioned over the previous two centuries, from an ancient pitchfork to a newly purchased compression-driven double-barrelled pesticide gun. Gardening magazines, largely unread, and seed catalogues from every imaginable source lay scattered about, and pots and packets of seeds and tubers lined the drooping shelving. One shelf had completely collapsed, its former contents stacked randomly in the corner. Pinned in the gap left by the shelf was a damp and mouldering picture, torn from a magazine, of Geoff Hamilton smiling an encouraging smile.

A full ten minutes later, De'Ath spoke. "Well, it must be God, mustn't it?"

"What must, lad?" Bullock had completely forgotten the subject of De'Ath's meditation.

"Or Jesus. 'And I pray thee, loving Jesus that as Thou hast graciously given me to drink in with delight the words of Thy knowledge, so Thou wouldst mercifully grant me to attain one day to Thee, the *fountain of all wisdom* and to appear forever before Thy face.' The Venerable Bede, I believe, last words of 'Ecclesiastical History of the English People'."

"The Venerable Bede, eh?" reflected Bullock. "Was that, the Venerable Bede from Leeds, who ate a packet of seeds?"

"Well, the ancient priestly scholar came from Jarrow, Tyne and Wear, actually, but do continue, you know I like a good limerick." De'Ath sat back to listen with an expressionless face.

"Very well, my friend, I shall," said Bullock, blue eyes twinkling with humour. "The Venerable Bede from Leeds, ate a packet of seeds, and what came to pass, grass grew from his ass, and his balls...were *covered* in weeds."

De'Ath hooted (literally, like a tawny owl) with laughter. Bullock joined in with his own gravelly laugh. De'Ath slapped his thighs, another of his literal characteristics of mirth.

"Which is, of course, Thomas, what our patch is covered with." The two found this even funnier, and as they found each other's laughter amusing, the hooting and gravelling continued for some time.

"Oh, dear," spluttered Bullock, wiping a tear from his eye, "we do 'ave a laugh, lad. Eh up, new boots? Very smart, very smart."

De'Ath sobered up. "Yes, they are new. Dot bought them for me for Christmas. And that old lunatic that gardens the patch across the brook, he was all for putting his new fork through them!"

"Really?" asked Bullock, leaning forward, with a serious expression.

"Indeed. I made the mistake of wishing him Happy Christmas, and the next thing I know he's chasing me down the lane."

"Well I never. I know the fellow you mean. Very taciturn, looks a bit like Albert Steptoe."

"That's him."

"I've had a run in with him an' all. Just after I've started here, like, I've brought t'dog wi' me, not thinking on. Reet art o' bushes e' war. 'No dogs here he goes, read your rules of tenancy.' Well, fair play, he's right like, but he put me back up with 'is gamekeeper's attitude. And Basker was reet put 'art. Then next minute he's tellin' me 'ow to garden. 'Keep the hoe busy, he goes, keep the hoe sharp.' Owd claptrap. No bloody need for hoes these days. I told him. But he carried on poking about. Tried to come in t'Shed he did. He had his eye on some of these old tools, you know."

"Better keep our eyes on him then, Ron. Care in the Community, I reckon."

"Aye, we will, Tom. We will. Any roads up, I've done a lot of reading over Christmas, a lot. Titmarsh, Thrower, the lot. All of 'em. Smith, Hamilton, the lot. Research, I've done, lad, research. Just like me hero."

"Sherlock?"

"Aye lad, I'm a proper gardenin' Sherlock Holmes, Dr. Watson, unravelling the mysteries of the soil! See, there's this big debate about organic versus chemicals. Nature versus science. And I don't know which is reet. Listen to this for example." Bullock picked up a leaflet entitled "Organic Soil Care". He removed a pair of thick-framed spectacles from his top pocket, which De'Ath thought had an air of Eric Morecambe about them. Bullock cleared his throat, and began to read out the leaflet with unnecessary empahisis.

"Ahem. 'Soil care is the cornerstone of organic gardening. A fertile soil is one with both a good structure and a good supply of plant foods. Feed the soil not the plant. Use bulky organic manure. Make your own compost.' Now that sounds like sound advice to me, eh, Tom?"

"Well, of course, we did purchase that load of manure from the local stables. We were going to dig that in, were we not?" answered De'Ath, who was studying the leaflet handed to him by Bullock.

"Aye, c'mon, let's have a look at how this frost is breaking that hoss muck down".

The novice gardeners heaved themselves from their seats with great sighs and exiting the Shed, eyed their patch with concern. A rather poor attempt at digging over about a quarter of the ground had been made, and a pile of horse manure delivered in November lay in an undisturbed heap.

"Oh bollocks, I really thought we'd done more than this, Tom". Bullock paced the patch with a forlorn air.

"Plenty of time, Ron! Still lots of winter left".

"Aye...but seems like everybody else has got their plots dug. These 'ave 'ead start on us two latecomers. I'll tell thee what though, Thomas," Bullock patted his friend's bony shoulder with his gloved hand. De'Ath stood stiffly mid-allotment, being patted. "Ah say, I'll tell thee what, Thomas," said Bullock rather impatiently, patting De'Ath harder, jolting De'Ath's rickety frame.

"Oh, what, sorry, what will you tell me, Ron?" De'Ath coughed in reply.

Bullock moved his face to within an inch of De'Ath's and

held him firmly by both shoulders. He grinned and nodded as he quietly spoke. "I have a plan which will turn t' barren soil we see before us today into the most fertile soil this side of the Nile delta. In one month." Bullock took a step back, raising an index finger. "One month."

De'Ath regarded his friend's thrusting jaw and bulging eyes calmly. He took several pulls on his pipe before replying, and shortly before doing so, began to stroke his wispy light grey beard, which he did when becoming anxious. "I suspect you mean chemical nitrate powders, Mr. Bullock. I am afraid that I cannot endorse that approach. I do currently believe organic gardening to be the way of the past, *and* of the future."

"Well…mebbe you be right, or mebbe you be wrong, but I respect your opinion as a recently made, but nevertheless esteemed friend. And you will be pleased therefore to learn that my solution is 100% organic." Bullock raised one hand in triumph at this last point.

"Well, let us learn more of this in the warmth of our den, sir," said De'Ath, rather pompously.

Back in the Shed, they resumed their punctured armchairs. Bullock leaned forward in his and began his proposal.

"What the farmers do, y'see Tom, is they bloody well bombard their land with all the shite they can get their 'ands on. All the shite, collected over the winter, in the pigsheds, in the cattle barns, in the chicken pens, they get this evil brew they call slurry, and they get it, and they pump it on t'fields. You smell it in the spring, lad. It's evil stuff. But by

Christ, does it fertilise. It is pure, liquid, plant food, Tommy. No digging in a bit of hoss poo for them, old lad! And old Ronny here has pulled off a bit of a coup. Because I have secured... only if you are in agreement, mind... a slurry tank full of this material for use on our own humble plot. One of my lad's mates is a farm worker, y'see, Wallo, he's called, and I was talking to him about this int' boozer. He was telling me all about it. Now, strictly speaking, you can't use this stuff on allotments, but I says to him, there's a ton says, where there's a will there's a way. And he says, for a ton, he will pump our land with the good stuff, no worries, no questions asked. Now, what do you reckon?"

At this, there was a lengthy pause in conversation, as both leaned back in their armchairs and smoked furiously. The air became so thick with smoke they could no longer see each other. At length, De'Ath spoke. "Seems plausible. Raw sewage though, Ron. Bit of a health hazard?"

"Long as we dig it in, no problem. The soil just breaks it up. And I'll tell you something else this lad told me an' all. Human urine. Best plant fertilizer in t' world. Pisses on his sunflowers, he tells me, and they grow ten foot. Spray it about, he says. Even if you want a dump, let it go t'land. Look at the Chinese. Shit in the pond, carp eats shit, Chinese eat carp. Can a billion Chinese be wrong?"

"Hmmm, looks a bit fishy, doesn't it, fouling one's nest as't were."

"We could rig summat up. A Portaloo, direct t'soil."

De'Ath drew himself up from his armchair and stretched. "Mr. Holmes, I can find no fault in this plan. I'm all for the recycling of waste. I'm all for the organic. And this plot clearly needs some intensive manuring. As long as we are careful with our programme, this should be a very interesting experiment. Now, I feel a call of nature approaching. Let us construct a Portaloo, as you put it, from these old tarpaulins."

"I like your style, Tommy boy."

Two hours later, after much banging and clattering, they manoevered a flimsy object resembling a giant box kite from the Shed and set it in the middle of the plot. Bullock was very pleased with the result. He entered via a hinged entrance.

"Bigger than you think inside, Tom. We could call it "The Turdis". This amused Bullock enormously, and he began a chesty laugh. Very few of the people in Bullocks's life had been able to forgive the Yorkshireman's trait of finding his own jokes the funniest of all, but De'Ath could. More than this, he found Bullock's laughter always infectious, and could rarely help his own wheezy owlish laughter in the face of it. By happy accident, Bullock also found the sight and sound of De'Ath in mirth a reinforement of his own. Thus, like two adolescents, Bullock's red face peeping occasionally at De'Ath from behind the screen door like a demented Dr. Who, the pair spent many minutes in helpless laughter. "The Turdis!" Bullock kept repeating, whipping up further gales of hooting mirth.

The old man with the fork looked out on the comedians with disdain. Donald Philp had gardened on Oldside Allotment for the best part of fifty years. He had seen them come and seen them go. Usually, a man took an allotment, worked it for a couple of seasons, then lost interest or moved. He presumed that De'Ath and Bullock would fall into this category. He was especially contemptuous when two jobsworths had arrived to install the red cedar box shed on De'Ath's plot. "Bloody garden centre special," he had muttered under his breath, as he retreated to his own ancient shed for a brew.

Philp's shed seemed to have grown from its own seed from the earth, so part of the allotment landscape did it look. Bullock's Shed had been the den of an old friend who had died a year or so ago, and Philp had spent many an hour in there. Like his own, it was full of the wisdom of the tribal elder, a place where secrets had passed. He was disposed to mentor Bullock on his arrival, who seemed much impressed by the homespun qualities of his Shed, but Philp quickly realised that the only wisdom Bullock was interested in was his own.

Philp liked his own company well enough, and was happy to be separated from Bullock and De'Ath's allotment by a hedge and a brook. His wife had died many years ago, yet he still missed her when he went back to his terraced house, so he spent much of his time on his allotment or in his shed, where he found peace. Always a competent gardener, on retirement, Philp had become a local gardening legend. He had an informal role with the Parish Council to oversee the allotments to see that the few local rules were not breached, but in his capacity as warden, he was more familiar as a dispenser of advice. Most were happy to listen and learn.

Bullock and De'Ath had six months ago taken adjoining allotments at around the same time, both having recently retired. Both had taken up long-held ambitions to take up gardening as a serious hobby, and both were anxious to be out from under their wives' feet. Slowly, they became friendly as pipe-smoking aficionados, spending more and more time in the Shed, and doing very little gardening.

They had agreed to join forces, by pooling their allotted land. De'Ath had gladly abandoned the "Cedar Box", transferring his few tools and setting up den in Bullock's Shed.

This seemed reasonable enough to Philp, but all they seemed to do was smoke and lark about, like two middle-aged truants. Not what the gardening ethic was about at all, he thought. He had tried again with Bullock, explaining before the winter that they would have to give the plot a real digging over, as it had been neglected awhile. Bullock had scowled petulantly.

"We're not novices you know, Mr. Philp. Come and see my lawn sometime old lad!" Bullock had exclaimed.

"Well, I'll leave you old hands to get on with it then," Philp had shrugged, walking away.

Philp watched them now, fooling about. They seemed to have constructed a mobile hide. "Perhaps they are taking up bird-watching," he thought, as he began to trudge home.

"They'll be bored and gone by spring."

"Oh, come in, love. Lovely to see you. Sit down in there, I'll put the kettle on. GET DOWN, BASKERVILLE!"

Bella took her friend's thick woollen coat and hung it from a brass hallway coathanger in the shape of an ivy trellis. She dragged a drooling aged bloodhound by its collar and confined it behind the kitchen door.

"How was your Christmas Day, Dot?"

"Oh lovely, thanks, Bella. Tommy loved his boots. And how was your busy day?"

"I am absolutely exhausted. Sit down, come on. Do you want one, Dot?" Bella offered an Embassy, as always; Dorothy refused, as always. The ladies sat in easy animated conversation by the replica coal fire, in huge, settee-sized chairs.

"Well, fifteen people for Christmas lunch! Would you ever? But Ron would insist. 'I want all my family this year, he says. For me retirement. We'll all muck in.' Muck in? 'Course, nobody did. Ron played everybody at chess until he'd beaten everyone, and well, you can't expect the foreigners to help with turkey."

Bella could not explain how, as a self-confessed racist deeply influenced by Enoch Powell's "Rivers of Blood" speech of 1968, that three of her four offspring had married 'foreigners'. In fact, her son Ray had married an English girl of Indian parents, although Surinda's claims to be British met with incredulity from Bella. Her eldest son, Geoff, lived in France and had married a dusky Bretagne called Angeline. Bella despised the French. "But how can I criticise mixed marriages, me from Lancashire?" she would laugh with her daughters-in-law, "I married a bloody foreigner meself! 'Marrying a Yorkie' me poor old dad exclaimed, 'may as well marry a darky!'"

And much to Bella's astonishment and exasperation, Bella's daughter Wendy had married a 'darky'. She had returned from a three-week holiday to Hawaii with a deep tan, half a dozen grass skirts for her friends and mother, and twenty-two stones' worth of Fijian husband. Bella had been appalled but resigned, Bullock had instantly christened the genial Ranatunga 'Jonah Lomu', and organised a 'proper' wedding reception for the following month. "Bad enough," he announced, "that my youngest daughter gets married on Honolulu beach, without my permission to a savage with a bone through his nose! But I'll be beggered if I don't get to make a speech!" And speech he had made, an epic of fifty-two minutes, mainly about the murder of Captain James Cook by Hawaiian natives.

Bella referred to her six inter-racial grandchildren, two from each marriage, as her 'Piccaninnies.' Bullock would croon in club singer style, Blue Mink's hit of 1969 '*What we need is a great big meltin' pot...'* whenever they were about, which they all loved. Bella was not a fan of the melting pot concept of inter-racial mix, but was a loving, if forthright, grandmother.

"It's so lovely that our boys get on, Bella. I wasn't at all sure how Tommy would cope with his early retirement. I thought he'd be hanging around the house a lot."

"Yes, Ron doesn't have a lot of friends you know, Dot. Knows everybody, but few friends. Likes it that way, he says. And he does like your Tommy... well, they don't say, men, do they, but I can tell. Tom could not wait to retire. He was like a kid on summer holidays the day he came home. Straight up t'wardrobe, came down with his business suits, and said 'Off to Oxfam with them buggers, Bel, I'm done with repping forever. I'm sixty-two, worked since ah were sixteen, now ah'm havin 20 years off then sitting on a bloody cloud next to you for the next thousand.' He could not wait to retire." Bella chuckled and shook her head fondly.

"Did he plan to take up gardening then, Bella?"

"Well, not really, that was out of the blue, as far as I know. I mean look at our garden, he was never bothered. Apart from the lawn." The ladies looked through the French windows to the garden beyond. Larch lap fencing enclosed three sides of the garden, a ragged conifer hedge on two, and a large, bright green lawn was at the centre. A flagstone path meandered the lawn with, at regular interludes, eccentric stone statues.

"He was always pretty disparaging of the gardening programmes, especially that one where they change people's gardens. 'Just look at what they've done to that poor bugger's lawn, Bella. Just come and look at this. They've made a bloody gravel grotto. Look at him pretending he likes it!!' Oh, he went on and on."

She took a deep draw from her cigarette, before exhaling her next sentence with a stream of blue smoke.

"Oh, but the lawn. 'A mark of a man, his lawn, Bella,' Ron says. Likes to get those stripes in it, and woe betide a dandelion. Bumpipes, he calls them. Straight out with the herbicide. But you've a nice garden Dot, does Tommy do that?"

"Well, he helps. I'm the gardener really. I like cottage gardens, you know, herbs and wild flowers."

"Yes, I'd like more flowers. Perhaps now I'm married to Percy Thrower I'll get some grown. You know though, love, it's not gardening they're interested in really. It's that Shed. That's what they do, you know. Sit in t'Shed smoking and laughing."

"Really?"

"Aye, Wendy went down to see her dad the other weekend, you've not met Wendy yet, have you Dot?" Bella went to the shelves next to the mantlepiece, and removed a portrait of a girl in college graduation robes. There's me clever girl, she went to college at the University of Luton. Oh we were proud that day, Dot, when she got her degree. Do you know who presented it to her? Rita off Coronation Street. See, there's a picture of me with Rita, look!"

Bella was about to fetch a photograph album of the day, but suddenly remembered that her new friend had no children of her own, and changed conversational tack.

"Anyway, aren't people who go on about their own children boring. I want to know all about your Christmas, come in kitchen while I make tea."

"Oh, I like hearing about your family, Bella. So many of you, it's hard putting all the pieces in place!"

In the kitchen, Baskerville lay dejected in his basket, raising only an eyelid to watch the ladies prepare tea. He heard the biscuit barrel open with its familiar pop, but recognised only the rustling sound and then the smells of wafer biscuits. Wafers. He hated wafers. No point getting out of his box for a bit of wafer.

"Poor old Baskerville," said Bella, stroking his ears. "The only problem with that allotment is they don't let dogs on. Come on outside, Basker, and chase these squirrels off."

"Squirrels," he thought. He nearly caught one once. He remembered that. Caught it by the tail. Then it got away. In his dreams though, the squirrels did not get away. He would shake them by the neck like the rats they were.

"Come on Basker...ATTACK!" encouraged Bella loudly, opening the back door.

"Attack," he thought. "Bark, run fast. What the heck, I will."
There was no chance of Baskerville catching a squirrel these
days, but as he lolloped out of the back door, he scattered
a couple of them from the lawn where they were stealing
the bread that Bella had thrown out for the birds. He felt
good about dismissing them from his domain, and went
to water the stone statue of a Chinese lion, in celebration.

"That's an unusual name, Baskerville. Is it to do with the
Hound of the Baskervilles?" asked Dot, delicately biting a
sliver of wafer and sipping from her teacup gracefully.

"Oh yes, Dot", coughed Bella, laughing as she gulped her
tea from a mug with Bolton Wanderers Football Club and
a cartoon lion on it. "It most certainly is. Come with me."

Bella led Dot through the lounge and into a study.
"Thomas's great hero is Sherlock Holmes, Dot. Ever since
he was a boy, apparently. She pointed to the shelves.
Complete works of Conan Doyle. Deerstalker hat. Even a
magnifying glass, look. Ha, ha". She held the lens to her
face, moving it to and fro, until her bloodshot eye was the
size of a saucer. Dot burst into laughter.

"Oh, you're a case, Bella!"

As they moved back to the kitchen, Bella wheezed and
coughed a smoker's cough, still laughing.

"She looks older than her years" thought Dot, "I think she
has had a hard life somewhere back. I'll ask her one day. I
like her very much."

"So now I see, Bella, the carved pipes as well. Yes, I can see my Tommy as Dr. Watson."

"Well, I think they're taking this gardening too seriously. The dog doesn't get a look-in at the left overs anymore. And they are down there all hours. Tom went down in the middle of the night last night! Something to do with organic gardening."

"Spring can't be far away," thought De'Ath, as he squelched through the now muddy allotment track. January and half of February had passed in a uniform, windy grey passage of days, but now the sun shone with some warmth, and snowdrops and crocuses brought cheer and colour. De'Ath had returned from a long weekend at the coast and was looking forward to being on the allotment again. He was really enjoying himself. He felt youthful and purposeful. He was slightly taken aback, however, when he reached the patch. It resembled a waste tip, but smelled much worse. Food detritus - apple cores, orange peel, sodden cereals, large volumes of boiled rice, and even the remains of a Christmas cake - lay strewn around.

"GANGWAY WATSON!!!" came a cry from behind him. Bullock was tearing down the lane at high speed, resembling a dishevelled and geriatric prop forward. "No time for t'booth this fine morning!!" roared Bullock, as he breathlessly passed the startled De'Ath. On reaching their patch, Bullock ripped open his trouser flies and began to urinate in a wide arc on the ground. "Bloody 'ell only just med it," he panted to himself.

From up the path De'Ath was waving and shouting. "Ron, the train's coming!!"

Bullock shouted back over his shoulder, "Oh aye, nice one Tommy, that left, shall we see, eleven minutes ago!!"

It was true that the 'Tredbury Flyer', the commuter train that passed close by the allotment via an embankment, had a good record of punctuality for the era. But by no means was it a service to set a watch by. And it was not at all likely that De'Ath would attempt any kind of joke.

The train was late out of Oldside Station that day. Wendy Wakaya had become quite fond of seeing her father and his strange new friend on their allotment as the sun rose, whilst she commuted to work on the 8.05. "There he is!" she pointed out every morning to her fellow travellers, "digging for England!" Like her father, Wendy enjoyed the irony of repetition far more so than her companions, especially fellow commuter Phillip Ward. Phillip was not conversational in a morning and liked to read the paper and drink polystyrene-flavoured coffee in peace. Wendy's recent habit of encouraging the whole carriage to wave at her father was beginning to grate. He raised his newspaper high as the train approached the allotments, but Wendy was persistent. "There he is, wave everyone…oh, come on Philip, wave! Aaah, there he is…oh my God!…DAD?!!!!"

Phillip peered sleepily over The Daily Telegraph. "What's your father doing? Oh, today he's *weeing* for England,

Wendy! Why is his mate putting that box-kite on his head? Oh look, he's pissed on his friend!!"

It was true that the gardening duo were in some disarray. "Get that bastard off me, you berk!!" yelled Bullock.

"Just trying to protect your modesty from the commuters, Ron," panted De'Ath.

"They'd never 'ave seen me todger, ah've got me back t'train. That's Stephen bloody Byers' fault that is. Bloody late trains." Finally zipping up his flies, Bullock trudged glumly for the Shed, an irrigated De'Ath dragging the Manuring Booth (as it was now more decorously called) behind him.

De'Ath filled an old kettle from a standing tap, and Bullock lit a camping stove in the Shed, using the Davidoff Prestige Lighter given to him as his retirement present.

"Allotment looks a bit of a sight, Ron, where did all that rubbish come from?" asked De'Ath, entering the Shed.

"Oh, ah've 'ad all me family save up their food waste and drop it this weekend. I were waitin' for you to come back and help dig it in. Y' see Wallo pumped the slurry in as I instructed. Careful how you go out there, it's still soaking in. Stinks a bit, but it'll soon settle."

Wallo had indeed soaked the allotment patch in farm slurry the previous night. He had been very careful to ensure that no one had observed him with his tanker. He realised that this was highly irregular, but a hundred pounds was a hundred pounds. He had agreed with Bullock to dig a hole in the middle of the plot, and had inserted the tanker hose into it. The slurry had oozed away, and Wallo was content that it would not be especially obvious the next morning that a couple of tonnes had been dispensed.

Ron and Tom pottered about, making two huge mugs of tea, and finally sat down. "Sorry I pissed on you there, Tom. I should not have doubted your alarm call."

"Perfectly alright on both counts, old chap".

"Eh, why was the tomato blushing?"

"Hmmm, I think I know this one." De'Ath liked to try to work out punchlines of jokes, to the annoyance of most, but not to Bullock, who always allowed him as much time as he wanted to solve the puzzle.

"Ahah, because it saw the salad dressing!" announced De'Ath in triumph, several minutes of furrowed-browed thought later.

"Nope, because it was seen tekkin' a leek!" grinned Bullock. "Like me!!"

Both were amused by this, De'Ath being forced to cough tea out of his mouth onto his shirt. "Oh, blast, it isn't my day," he muttered.

"Now then, auld wet lad, I've summat to show thee. Ah've made a little plan of our plot." Bullock removed a folded piece of graph paper from his trouser pocket and, leaning forward in his armchair, smoothed it out on the floor of the Shed. De'Ath too leaned forward to inspect the paper.

Bullock began explaining the various coding and many arrows of what seemed a complex piece of landscape design.

"So I've got t'spuds over here, earlies here, lates there. Bean patch over there. Cabbage and caulies, big as footballs there. Aye, and broccoli too. And perhaps a flower bed. You know, pinks, carnations mebbe."

"Hmmm, yes. Seems sensible. I rather thought I'd grow some squashes and strawberries."

"Excellent, yes," encouraged Bullock. "Nice straw mats down here, with some netting, eh?"

Throughout the morning, the plans went on, getting ever more adventurous. Finally, the graphic had been amended thoroughly, and both sat back satisfied, with loaded pipes, each with a contented vision of how well the allotment would look come summer.

"Excellent, Watson. Now, let's get the seed catalogues. Just wait until that codger Philp sees what can be done with proper manure." A large list of obscure seed varieties were listed, and pinned to the wall of the Shed, next to the complicated 'Patch Plan'. "Well we'd better be getting on with the digging old son," announced Bullock. "Hang on, is that the time? Time for lunch, mate!"

"Do believe it is, Ron. Digging'll have to wait!!"

They sat down again. Bullock produced a miner's pail, which had belonged to his father. Within, wrapped roughly in kitchen roll, were half a pork pie, some slices of black pudding, a tomato, a gherkin, a Kit-Kat and a sports bottle of Vimto cordial. From an ancient canvas walker's rucksack, De'Ath produced a Tupperware box. He carefully arranged its contents on the upturned lid: a fresh linen serviette, salt and pepper pots, two hard-boiled eggs, triangular-cut tinned salmon sandwiches and a tin of ginger beer.

Bullock flicked a switch on an old Roberts radio. "Your turn today, Thomas, I believe it is." He tuned it to the Radio 4 World at One. Bullock was a 5-Live fan, De'Ath a Radio 3 or Radio 4 man. They accommodated each other's preferences by alternating days. But they both looked forward to listening to the cricket in the summer on Radio 4 long wave, although Bullock felt it wasn't the same without Freddie Trueman, and De'Ath would have paid large sums of money to hear John Arlott just once again. They listened to the news, without comment, but with many tuts and shaking of heads.

With a large belch, Bullock announced that lunch was over. "Eh, Tom, have you heard of the garlic diet?"

"Hmmm, the garlic diet. Something to do with vampires is it, or bad breath, perhaps?"

"The latter. You don't lose much weight, but from a distance your friends think you look thinner."

De'Ath nodded. "Yes, it can play optical tricks, distance."

"Chuck the leftovers out, eh Tom?" he said, throwing a pork pie crust out onto the litter-strewn plot.

"This is the bloody life. A mug of tea and a pipe, old chap?"

"Oh, I think so, Ron."

Another half hour passed contentedly. "Well we'd better be getting on with the digging auld son, I suppose", said Bullock, reluctantly. They stood up, putting their jackets on rather slowly.

Just then it began to rain lightly. The rain made a delightful drumming sound on the corrugated metal roof. "One of my favourite sounds of all, that is," announced Bullock, "along with the tide ebbing on a pebble beach. How about you, what about your favourite sounds?"

"That is a damned good question, Ron," replied De'Ath, sitting down again. "Perhaps you would allow me a bowl in contemplation of my answer?"

"Aye, that is your perogative, my good doctor," replied Bullock, also sitting again. "And I will join you in a bowl of my own tobacco, whilst I enter a reverie to ask myself the following related question. What are my least favourite sounds?"

They sat in smoking silence for several minutes, as the rain pattered musically above them.

"Knitting needles clicking together, and the gong for dinner at a hotel I frequent on the Dorset coast," De'Ath had suddenly announced.

Bullock nodded sagely. "Nokia mobile ring tones, babies crying on a bus, equal first bad sounds."

They both sat entranced by the sound of the rain. Bullock stretched out in his legs and sighed. The pitter-patter of the raindrops had a soporific effect on him. His eyelids began to droop, and he cupped his hands in his lap to prepare for the sleep that was coming to him. De'Ath sat for some minutes reading his gardening catalogue, but for him too, sleep seemed an entrancing proposition. A couple of minutes later, the catalogue slipped from his hands, and he was in the land of what he still called Nod.

It was the foetid smell on the wind that attracted Philp to Tom and Ron's plot that afternoon. His nose wrinkled in disgust at the sight beholding him. "Jesus, what a dump!" Philp declared out loud. He was well known for talking to himself. He gingerly tested the soil with his fork. "Oh dear me, this is worse than when the gypsies set up camp. Time for a word with those buggers, Donald."

Noticing the Shed door was closed, Philp knocked lightly. You didn't just barge into another man's shed, even if that man was turning his allotment into a cross between a landfill site and a septic tank. He thought he could hear the sound of snoring, and knocked again. "Come out, I want a word." Still nothing stirred. He went round the side of the Shed, and pressed his wizened old face to the nearly opaque window.

At that moment, De'Ath was coming round from a dream of creatures of the deep. His eyes slowly opened and focused. "AAAAAAAARRGGGHH!!!!" he yelled, involuntarily. He was mid-way between sleep and wakening, as a green, scaly face peered at him from outside.

Bullock awoke with a start and leapt to his feet. "What the…"

De'Ath was pointing to the face at the window.

"PHILP!! What the hell are you doing spying on us!" Bullock yanked open the door, and Philp marched round, green algae all over his right cheek.

"Were you buggers asleep?" he growled.

"Yes, sorry Mr. Philp, I thought you were a sea monster, you see, I was dreaming…" De'Ath began apologetically, but Bullock interrupted him.

"What bloody business is it of yours if we were sleeping or having a violin recital?"

Philp realised that he should not have been peering through their window and that he had lost the high moral ground. "Yes, look, sorry, er, can I come in? I just want a word."

"No, you cannot come in," insisted Bullock angrily. "What the hell is that on your boots?"

Something nasty was indeed sticking to the soles of his wellies. Philp became animated again. "That is just the reason I've come to see you!! You're not turning this allotment into a dump. Either garden here or give it up!"

Bullock was momentarily speechless. "A dump? You daft beggar, can't you see we're manuring? Just wait till you see what comes off here this season!"

"Well whatever you've got here, it wants rotting and digging in!" Philp exclaimed.

"Listen, Philp, you garden the old ways and me and Thomas'll do it our ways. We'll see at the end of the season who gets it right."

"I'll give you till next Friday. If your plot is in this foul mess next week, you're out boyo!"

Philp righteously marched off across the plot. It seemed to him though, and also to Ron and Tom watching his progress, that the earth beneath him was moving. Philp strode on, thinking that this was a little like walking on an upland peat bog, where the peat often 'floated' on a layer of water. Indeed, this was exactly the case. The slurry pumped in the previous evening had formed a shallow, subterranean lake beneath pods of soil. In places the pod was thin, and not capable of sustaining human weight, even a light man like Donald Philp. One moment the ancient gardener was striding belligerently across the plot, the next moment, with a shriek, his legs disappeared from view.

"Oh 'eck," said Bullock quietly.

Philp was up to his shoulders in foul, greenish-black ooze, being in the hole that Wallo had dug as a funnel for his slurry delivery. Philp seemed to be in no danger of actually disappearing, but that was not his own impression. "AAAGHHH, QUICKSAND! QUICKSAND!!" he wailed.

"Don't get too near, Tommy," cautioned Bullock, "this is just like one of those old Tarzan films. Cheetah used to bring a long vine at this point and Ron Ely would pull himself out."

"GET ME OUT OF THIS SHIT HOLE NOW!" ordered Philp, as the two fellows above him gingerly tested the soil.

"Go and grab the big rake, Tommy, that should reach him."

De'Ath ran swiftly to the Shed, whilst Bullock tried unsuccessfully to keep Philp calm, as he was beginning to lash out at his murky imprisonment. "Keep calm, Swamp Thing!" encouraged Bullock.

De'Ath arrived with the rake, which he proffered towards Philp.

"Hang on, Swamp Thing...heave, Tommy!"

Philp was hauled like a soiled amphibian from the mire to drier land, where he lay dejected. Before he knew what was happening, he was being hosed down with freezing water by Bullock. He staggered to his feet, Bullock grimly training the hose on the old man. "Got to get this stuff off you, auld chap," shouted Bullock over the spray, "or you'll stink like a pig for t' rest of the year."

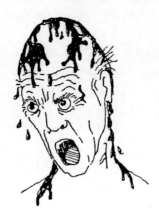

The standpipe hose did its work well, and Philp stood, stunned, cold and soaked. "What…what are you pillocks up to?!" shrieked Philp. "I've never had anything like this happen to me in sixty years of gardening. What…what the hell is that stuff?!"

"Liquid manure, Mr. Philp," explained Bullock stern and unrepentant, "we give it a good dousing last night. You shouldn't be walking about on our plot."

Philp was too staggered to argue and decided to get home before he froze. "Get this bloody patch sorted quick. By next Friday. Or I swear I'll have you off!" He limped off, dripping.

As soon as Philp had wobbled away on his bike, Bullock burst into laughter. "Oh dearie me," he gasped, "I'll have to call him Swamp Thing from now on!! Dozy old fool!"

"Even so," replied De'Ath who was too shocked by events

to be amused, "Philp's got a point. I mean just look at the state of the place!"

"Aye, you are not wrong, it wants digging in."

"Let's get the spades straight away, eh?"

"Not ser fast, Thomas. I've had a better idea. Must have dreamed it up when I was asleep. Think technology, son. It would take us bloody hours digging by hand! Rotivator, boy! Motor rotivator!!"

"And where might we get such a device? GettaTool, perhaps?"

"Aye, and who's got a son-in-law working at GettaTool?"

"You have, Ron."

"Correct, sir. Tony. Useless get. I cannot understand why Sheila married him. It's about time he came in for some use. We shall pay him a call, doctor. You know my methods, Watson."

"It is a strange experience shopping, nowadays, is it not, Thomas? I suppose Cash-and-Carry started all this."

De'Ath and Bullock were striding across a car park on a grey Saturday morning in middle England. On all sides were cavernous shopping warehouses. Pets R Us seemed quite popular, but it was impossible to park anywhere near Do-it-Right. As they neared their destination, GettaTool, the four-feet high pink lettering against lime green hoardings bade them enter the "Giant Sale" that had been on for at least five months. Entering by a temperamental automatic door, they entered a cavernous warehouse expanse, with an incredible range of machine tools on display, each with a star-shaped luminous yellow board displaying the name and rental price of each item. Two fifteen-year old youths in pink and lime green aprons were scrumming over a plastic cup in the 'Information' kiosk.

De'Ath and Bullock waited, uncharacteristically patiently for the latter, for the youths to attend to them, but in vain. Bullock entered the kiosk, grabbed the cup and punted it into a nearby cement mixer. The youths, reddened by their mêlée, straightened and looked at Bullock blankly. Both had shaven heads, one of them had a ring through his eyebrow, the other had shaved off his eyebrows entirely.

"See that, two points that were…not bad for a backrow forward, eh? Now, where's Mr. Howkins?"

"Er, who's Mr. Howkins?" offered one of the youths, who went immediately puce upon speaking.

"Tony Howkins?"

The youths exchanged vacant glances.

"Tony Howkins, deputy manager of Oldside GettaTool, my son-in-law and I presume somewhere in the hierarchy, your boss. Perhaps you would go and seek him out, unless it's time for you to scrum down again?"

"Oh, sorry, yeah? We only work on Saturdays, yeah? I'll try and find him, yeah? Hold the fort, Donut."

De'Ath had drifted off to inspect an industrial sander, and Donut and Bullock were left to intergenerational inspection of one another. "Do you like rugby then, lad?"

"It's alright."

"You want to be playing proper rugby for the school on a Saturday."

"We don't do rugby."

"Oh."

"Football is it? All football these days, eh?"

"We don't do football. In the winter."

"What do you mean, you don't do football in the winter? What do you do in the winter then?"

"Games."

Bullock shook his head. "It's no bloody wonder we can't beat the Aussies at 'owt," he muttered, and wandered off.

De'Ath was inspecting a box-like piece of equipment. "I'm blowed if I can figure out what this is supposed to do, Ron! Can you make it out?"

Bullock lowered himself down to his knees, and peered beneath the box, his face turning purple and his neck folds flopping over his chin. "Well, there is a hose," reported Bullock. He got to his feet, brushing his hands together. "I believe, Watson, this instrument to be a Suburban Noise Box."

De'Ath stood dumb-founded. "A what?" he replied, his hands on his hips, or rather, his ribs. Whenever De'Ath assumed the hands-on-hip stance, his hands were braced nearer his armpits than his waist.

"The Suburban Noise Box, Doctor, is a fiendish invention. It has no practical use, but serves two purposes. You plug him in, throw that switch yonder, and by crikey, it makes a din!"

"And the reason for the din, sir, is…"

"The din is the end in itself, sir. Imagine, Thomas, it is a lovely day in your suburban garden. Yes, the birds are singing, and as it is the Sabbath day, you are sitting out on the patio, and your missus comes out with a nice mug of tea and 'The Telegraph'. You sit, in quiet contentment. Then, from down the road, it starts. The first electric lawnmower. Then the perpetual builder sets up his axle-grinder. The prat opposite with the awful toddler comes out braying about toilet training. The feller next door starts his electric hedge trimmer. Over the road a chainsaw starts up. The stench of the barbeque begins. And so on. Until the song of the birds is drowned out by the cacophony of power tools and the air is full of suburbanite prattle and the smell of burning sausage! Now, there is nothing more for it! Bring forth the Suburban Noise Box!"

De'Ath had shifted his position to one of contemplation. His left hand supported his right elbow as his right hand stroked his wispy beard, and he gazed into the distance, recognising well the picture painted, and he grimaced as it was composed.

Bullock continued his fancy with gusto. He mimed the hauling of the large box onto the lawn. "There. To the far end of the garden with it. That's it. Now, switch on. RRRRRRAAAAHHHHRRRR!!!, it goes." Bullock stood vindicated, looking victoriously around his neighbourhood. "There you buggers. Cop some of that racket!"

"So, it serves no other purpose than adding to the noise pollution of the district," said De'Ath, thoughtfully.

"Nay, lad," responded Bullock, gleefully, "gives *you* the upperhand. And there's more strings to its bow. Somebody having a bonfire and spoiling yer washing? No bother. Whack an olt tyre in t'Noise Box, it'll burn it for thee. Direct the stench where you want it to go, with its fan here, look! Or owt you want…barbecue lighter fuel, creosote, pig shit, owt yer like, lad!!"

"So, it makes gratuitous noise and local air pollution. This is scandalous, Ron. What have things come to? But you did say it has two purposes. Assuming that proving you can be more of a social nuisance than your neighbours is one, what, pray, is the other?"

At this point, Bullock became more conspiratorial, and he lowered his voice and took De'Ath's arm. "Well, now. Imagine your missus has chucked you out of the house to slave in the garden. Right. Out with The Noise Box. You, down the local, the canal for a fish, or whatever you want. Come in, weary-looking, like. 'By 'eck, love,' you go, 'that's thirsty work farraping the lintels, eh? Nice cup of tea would be nice?' Missus goes 'Oh, you do deserve one, love, having to use that noisy thing. Sit down and have a rest, I'll put kettle on.' Bullock winked theatrically and chortled.

But De'Ath withdrew his arm. "Ron, this is a disgrace. This instrument is a device of pollution and deceit!"

Bullock knew well when to end the joke with his over-gullible friend. "Well, since you don't approve, Thomas, I can see you will not be in the market for one of these. But believe me, they will catch on. They are good for one more thing, an' all."

"And what would that be?"

"Kiddin' yer mates," replied Bullock with a twinkle of his blue eyes.

De'Ath was easily fooled, but was a wonderful recipient of a joke at his own expense. His arms fell to his sides in wonder, he smiled his beautiful smile and reddened slightly. He then held his head in his hands, picturing it vividly as an animated cartoon ass's head. He brayed to indicate that he felt like the donkey.

"Oh dear, oh dear," said Bullock, between gales of laughter,

"The Suburban Noise Box! Got you with that one, eh, lad!"

De'Ath could only nod, being now speechless with hooting laughter and braying.

"Mind you," said Bullock, suddenly becoming serious, "they might catch on one day, tha' knows."

His eye had been taken by a billboard propped next to the Information kiosk. "Blimey, Tom, come and look at this, there's a big picture of Tony here! Would you believe it, 'Employee of the Month' it says."

De'Ath came over to inspect the board. A lurid colour enlargement of a grinning fool shaking hands with a mustachioed grey-suited manager was set beneath a line of printed text which had originally read 'Tredley GettaTool Star Player of the Month.' However, a wag had neatly superimposed a label over 'Player, replacing it with 'Prat'.

"Tredley GettaTool Star Prat of the Month," read De'Ath. Bullock winced and peeled the label off with his thumbnail.

Tony waved from across the store, a genial Neanderthal in filthy overalls. Tony was the favoured butt of the many pranksters at large in the store, and today someone had managed a favourite one, by painting out the 'GETTA' from the store name badge on the back of his overalls. Tony strode towards his father-in-law with 'TOOL' emblazoned boldly across his back. "Hello dad, great to see you here! What can I do for you?" he said rubbing his hands together and grinning with the genuine enthusiasm of a simpleton.

"Hello, Tony. Well done on yer, er, award, there. Er, what did you win?"

Tony's grin widened even further. "Oh, yes, did you see that? Five times I've won it. None of the other lads seem to put their names up. You get a little medal."

"A medal? How pathetic," scowled Bullock, "think they'd give you a case of wine or something. No wonder nobody enters."

The smile on Tony's face drooped a little, leaving De'Ath rather sorry for him. A lot of people felt a bit sorry for Tony, and being a mothering soul, this was apparently enough reason for Bullock's daughter Sheila to have married him.

"Now, to business, Tony. Tek that silly smile off yer face. You know I've tekken up this gardening lark, eh? I am sharing this allotment with my new friend here, please meet Mr. De'Ath."

"Mr Death? You sound like a bag of laughs," grinned Tony.

"Well, he likes to pronounce it De'Ath, but it's spelt Death, in't it Tom?"

"No, no, not at all, it's De' Ath, Anglo Saxon origin, nothing to do with death at all, Ron. I thought you knew that, sorry." De'Ath shook his head, worriedly.

"He's just having a joke, Mr. De'Ath, you'll get used to, er, Mr. Bollock's sense of humour I'm sure. Wendy tells me you've taken to watering your allotment without a hosepipe, Dad. Certainly entertains the commuters, I hear?!" Tony began a high-pitched gulping laugh. Bullock did not respond with a laugh, but a pointed finger and a threat. The tortoise neck jutted forth.

"You can cut out that Bollock business...last man calling me that I knocked in t'middle o' next week, so watch it lad. And I'll piss all over you if you don't get us a good cheap rotivator." An edgy silence fell. Bullock was not one to take a joke at his own expense, and Tony was too stupid ever to remember it.

"A rotivator was it then Dad, was it? Come over here and have a look." Tony tried hard to restore an atmosphere of conviviality. "Don't want you watering me like one of your 'son-flowers', that's for sure, ha, ha..." His stupid remark instantly fell flat, and they all walked grimly on.

There were many rotivators to choose from. Bullock and De'Ath carefully tested each one. "They're all a bit flimsy," remarked Bullock.

"What's that one, Tony, over there?" enquired De'Ath.

"Oh that, the SSX-50, yeah, we've had some problems with that." Tony manoeuvred a large and complicated contraption off its blocks. "Yes, we have had some real problems with this one," grunted Tony "and at the moment I understand it's broken."

"Broken?" spat Bullock in disgust. "What's it doing in t' bloody showroom then? Get it down to our allotment tomorrow morning, and Tom and I will fix it for you free of charge. Can't say fairer than that. When you've serviced a Sherman tank, these lawnmowers are like Dinky toys. Eh, Thomas?"

"I can't do that, dad, the insurance..." mouthed Tony.

But Bullock had already turned, with De'Ath at his hip. Tony the Tool followed them out with words of mild protest, but they were as ineffectual as most of the machinery in the GettaTool showroom.

"Oh, bye the way, Tony," Bullock stopped in his tracks and pointed to the box-like machine which had been the subject of his comic speculations. "What is that contraption?"

"Oh, that," replied Tony with a smile of unwarranted pride. "New in from the States, dad. That's the Robotic Leaf Collector/Mulcher. Cool, huh?"

Bullock and De'Ath looked at each other with furrowed brows, with scorn at the polished box, and walked on wordlessly.

"I think on merit," muttered De'Ath at length, his arms jammed straight into their pockets as he loped, "that I preferred your fictitious SNB to the factual RLCM."

"Aye," agreed Bullock glumly. "These days, fact is certainly stranger than fiction."

As they strode back across the car park, Bullock had an idea. "Tell you what, son," he suggested to De'Ath, "whilst we're here, let's go and get us selves a nice bench from Do-it-Right. We need somewhere to sit outside the Shed when it gets nicer. They do cheapo garden furniture in there."

"Right you are, Ron, do you know, I've never been in there."

The pair entered the warehouse cavern, which swarmed with folk carrying pots of paint and planks of wood. "You there, my good man..." boomed Bullock to a tiny man in brilliant yellow overalls, who hurried away from them as fast as he could. "I say, you...bloody hell, he's run off! Come on, let's try and find someone else to help us!"

They searched for Do-it-Right staff in vain, but a full fifteen minutes later, found a long rack of elongated cardboard boxes, with a bench seat next to it. "Now then Tommy, look at this, this is what we want...thirty quid...can't say fairer than that, eh?" Bullock sat down hard on the pine seat, which squeaked and groaned. "Well, it is a cheapo job, but it'll do for t'plot eh? Have a sit on it, lad."

They both sat, testing the bench. They ascertained that it would just about do, and practised knocking out their pipes on the legs. "Eh up, staff!" remarked Bullock in surprise. A piggish woman with a complexion as yellow as her overalls trotted by. "Now then love, we'd like to have this one delivered please."

The pig woman stopped in her tracks. "Sorry sir, we don't do deliveries. And that is the demonstration model. The rest are behind you in boxes."

Both men peered behind them. "What, this is in one of these boxes? I don't believe you, they're not big enough!" remonstrated Bullock.

"I can assure you," answered the woman beginning to edge away, "it is all there in the box, instructions and everything. Even a little Allen key." She suddenly remembered a shard from her two-hour customer satisfaction induction briefing, conducted by a man in a cheap grey suit with even cheaper brown plastic shoes. She tapped her pocket. "Self-assembly. That way you get to save a little, we get to save a little!"

Bullock produced his wallet, which always contained at least fifty pounds. "Look here, my good woman, I am comfortably retired. We are not short of a bob, me and my mate here. I'll give you forty quid for this one here, and have my son-in-law pick it up later. How's that for you? You get to save a little bit more then, eh!" he said, winking at De'Ath, who sat passively as ever.

The woman shook her head, and wrinkled her snout. "That's not our policy, sir, I'm afraid. It's really easy though, I put one of them together myself last week." The woman hurried off without further word.

"Well, if she can do it, I'm sure we can manage to assemble

one of these things," announced De'Ath, rising. "Not being rude, but she looked just like a pig, that woman. Did you notice that, Ron?"

"Thought she was a fine looking woman, personally. Very rude, Tom, very rude. Never much good at woodwork me though, Tommo. Made a bookcase at school, though. Over to you for the project management. Come on then, let's get one of these buggers in t'car." Between them, they prised out from the rack one of the heavy boxes, and carried it to a queue of fully forty people waiting at the only staffed check-out aisle.

An hour later, back at the allotment, the contents of the box had been poured out at the rear of the Shed. There seemed to be an awful lot of small wooden pieces. Bullock was sorting through a plastic bag filled with an array of screws, dowels, a tube of wood glue and unidentifed metal and plastic objects. De'Ath was attempting to read a large page of diagrammatic instructions. "These just don't make sense, Ron," he announced at length. "The diagram doesn't make it at all clear which screws to use where."

"Give 'em here. Where are me glasses, here they are." Bullock squinted at the page, turning it left and right. "Well, are these written in Hebrew, or summat? Useless. Well, you know what they say, son, when in difficulty, read the instructions. Never mind, it can't be that tricky. Tell you what though," he said, picking up what appeared to be a bench leg, "it's a good bit of wood, this, give 'em credit."

"Yes, OK, let's make a start then. Now, we've got to glue these little wooden pegs in some of the holes. Which ones, I do not know."

An hour later, despite intense effort, the pile of wood was no nearer resembling a bench, and argument had begun to set in. "I told yer, Tommy boy, you cannot attach the side assembly until the seat slats are in place!!"

"I disagree. Look, the instructions clearly say…"

"The instructions? They are discredited man! They have been written to deliberately confuse!"

"OK, we'll do it your way. Seat slats last."

The men groaned and moaned for another hour, De'Ath petulantly humouring Bullock's increasingly desperate zeal. "By God, I'm ready for a cuppa, lad. But let's get these bastard screws tightened up. Now, where is that Allen key. Oh, bugger, I may have lost it in the grass. Tell you what, you get kettle on Tom, I'll search for it." Bullock nosed around in the long grass at the perimeter of the allotment. "Found it!" he announced triumphantly, as De'Ath emerged from the Shed with two mugs of tea. "Now then, let's tighten…oh, fuck it, it's bust! S'cuse my French. Bastard cheap rubbish."

"Well, it is starting to take shape," said De'Ath sipping at his tea.

"Yeah, the shape of a bloody sledge," responded the perspiring Bullock, gulping at his mug. "Eh, Tommy, Rosebud, eh? Did you see that film, Orson Welles. What was it called?"

"Citizen Kane. All the film buffs vote it their favourite-ever movie. I preferred the Third Man personally."

"Oh, aye, me too. Harry Lime, eh? Derderderderder, derder, derderderderder, derder…" Bullock broke into a broad grin, but De'Ath was staring into the middle distance. "Eh up 'es 'avin' a cogitation," said Bullock to himself, and sat down to finish his tea.

At length, De'Ath spoke, in an impossibly bad American accent. "In Italy for thirty years under the Borgias they had warfare, terror, murder and bloodshed but they produced Michelangelo, Leonardo da Vinci and the Renaissance. In Switzerland, they had brotherly love; they had five hundred years of democracy and peace and what did that produce?"

He looked at Bullock with his beautiful smile.

"The cuckoo clock! That is extraordinary recall, Tommy. You really should be on Mastermind…second thoughts, no, you'd be too slow. You'd only get one point." They both guffawed at this.

"I'll tell you what though, mate," said Bullock, pitching the dregs of his tea into the nettles, "we could do with a Third Man here! Especially if it was that handy man bloke off Changing Rooms…second thoughts, we wouldn't want a tosser like that on our patch!! Eh?"

"Lawrence Llewellyn-Bowen, is it?"

"No, no that's the poof. We certainly wouldn't want him on our patch. There's this Cockney macho man with a toolbelt. Fixes 'owt."

"I suspect before nightfall, Ron, we might need that man," said De'Ath, surveying the wooden carnage about them.

De'Ath was not wrong. It was almost dusk. The bench was nearing completion, but several spare pieces of wood, and many metal accessories, remained aside. "Right, this time, Tom. I'll hold it together, you press the seat slat piece in."

"I'm sure you shouldn't have tightened those screws fully before we do this, Ron."
"Well, I'm not bloody well untightening 'em now. It took me long enough with half an Allen key. Look, me thumb's all bleeding."

De'Ath began to apply pressure to the bench slats, attempting to force them into place within the assembly. "C'mon Tom, push!! It's soft wood, there's plenty of give in it!" De'ath pushed harder. There was a splintering noise as the assembly gave way. "BASTARD!!!" shouted Bullock very loudly.

"Rats." said De'Ath very quietly.

Bullock peered through the gathering gloom of the silent evening at De'Ath. "Do you know, Ron," said De'Ath, holding a fractured piece of wood in his hand, "at times like this, I feel like doing a Basil Fawlty…or even better, a Pete Townshend!"

"What, that bloke who used to smash up his guitars on stage?" replied Bullock, who was attempting to hold the remains of the frame together.

"Precisely."

Bullock thought for a moment. "Let's do it," he said quietly. For the next five minutes, the duo charged around the allotment, smashing the partly-assembled bench into smithereens. De'Ath took the backrest assembly, and beat it relentlessly against a tree trunk.
Bullock ripped the slats up, and threw them into a pile. "That … is … the … last … DIY … I … ever … bloody … do … it … meself!" he announced, rhythmically. After the cathartic carnage, they both lit a pipe, and sat on the ground, backs to the Shed, on the damp ground.

"Much nicer sitting on the earth anyway," ventured Bullock, unconvincingly.

The following morning at the allotment, Bullock and De'Ath were busy sprinkling the patch with large boxes of inorganic fertiliser, and other white nutrient powders. It looked for all the world as if a localised snowstorm had recently blown in. "In for a penny, in for a pound, Tom. Belt and braces. Just in case t' slurry don't work, this bloody will!" puffed Bullock, ripping the top from yet another carton of "GRO-MASSIVE".

De'Ath worked with a frown. He had reluctantly and temporarily dropped his objection to the use of synthetic fertilisers, being persuaded by Bullock that they needed to make up for lost time.

A Landrover and a trailer bumped down the lane and stopped at the gate of the allotment. Tony got out and waved enthusiastically. Bullock looked up scornfully. "Now then, looks like Tool is here. What on earth my Sheila saw in that man I will never know. Bloody hell, that rotivator looks bigger out here!"

"It is a monster," remarked De'Ath, as they walked towards the gate. With some difficulty, the three grappled the machine from the trailer using a ramp. The SSX-50 engine rotivator had been discontinued and recalled from sale some years ago by its manufacturer, following several complaints of erratic performance and safety problems.

"Now, this is a petrol engine hand plough, Dad, but it is seriously souped up. They don't make these any more," grunted Tony, wheeling it towards the plot.

Bullock inspected the machine through narrowed eyes. "Okay, Tony, start up the engine, I'll tune it."

Tony turned an ignition key, and a huge roar erupted from the engine, accompanied by plumes of blue smoke. By coincidence rather than foresight, Tony had two sets of ear protectors in the back of the Landrover, which he distributed. Putting the protectors on, De'Ath and Bullock were mutually transported to a National Service world of helicopter and tank maintenance, gesturing at each other mutely, and grinning.

"See you then, Dad, er, have fun, and give me a call when you want it picked up," yelled Tony, but he was ignored. He drove off disconsolantly.

During the next two hours, Bullock and De'Ath practically rebuilt the arcane gear system in the machine they had dubbed 'Arnie'. "Arnie, this is," grinned Ron, covered in grease and sweat, "you've heard of The Terminator, Tom…this is The Rotivator!"

"Arnie, yes, I like it. And he drove the fastest milk cart in the west. Now Arnie had a rival, an evil looking man…"

"No not Benny Hill, Tom, Arnie Schwarzenigger, eh, I've got it, Arnie Schwarzendigger! Ged'dit? Arnie Schwarzendigger?"

De'Ath got it, he liked it, and began a wheezy laugh. Soon they were both helpless with laughter. It took some time for them to get back to their re-engineering.

"Right, mate, Arnie's ready for battle. Now then, let's drag him into the corner of the patch, and let rip. You have first go. I want to see how deep he digs."

De'Ath started up the engine, it did sound quite silky.

"Purrs like a cat, Tommyboy. Den, der, der, der, der, der der der der derrrrr….."

"Whats that, Wagner?"

"No, no, Grand Prix Special…you know, Den, der, der, der, der, der der der der derrrrr….motor racing, Murray Walker…*and its Alain Prost in his McLaren*…Murray Walker…never mind, Thomas, let's get on with it."

De'Ath, with a maniacal grin, revved the engine with his right hand. Bullock winked back, giving the thumbs up and chocks away sign, as De'Ath engaged the clutch and selected gear. He assumed a braced position, legs astride, anticipating the pull of the engine.

But De'Ath's brace was considerably insufficient to hold back Arnie. De'Ath may have been a little jerky in letting out the hand-clutch, but in any event, large forces of forward propulsion were activated, and Arnie bucked wildly away. De'Ath resembled a water skier on his first lesson with a bad boat driver. For the first two seconds, he was hauled by his heels, and an arc of soil and detritus was sent spraying backwards via the speeding plough through his legs. Bullock was able to avoid the murky avalanche by diving headlong away, but the Shed was rained with filth. Bullock was surprised by this event, but not completely.

He knew that there was quite an engine in Arnie. But he was completely surprised when he looked up to see De'Ath now being hauled along face down and spread-eagled, hanging on to the handle. "LET IT BLOODY GO TOM!!" yelled Bullock. De'Ath had not heard this over the din of the engine, but had done so anyway. He lay shocked, filthy and immobile.

Though the events of the moment had surprised them both, they would have predicted the disengagement of the rotivator engine the moment De'Ath's grip on the clutch handles failed. To the great amazement of Bullock, now standing, Arnie continued not only to roar, but to plough on alone. And without De'Ath to hold it back, the over-souped machine careered on at a staggering speed. Leaving a single deep gorge in the allotment, Arnie veered and bucked down the gentle slope towards the brook.

What happened next was truly spectacular. De'Ath raised his head from the mire, but had no time to clean his glasses to see. Bullock's square jaw dropped in incredulity, as Arnie hit a rock on the bank of the brook, and somersaulted through the hedge on the far bank, the hawthorn hedge that marked the boundary of Donald Philp's allotment. As Arnie disappeared from view, the engine stalled, and there was half a second of terrible silence, before an almighty crash landing.

Bullock's legs were trembling as he lumbered towards De'Ath and hauled him to his feet. "Jesus, Thomas, I 'ope Philp has gone 'ome...Coom on!!"

They ran headlong across the footbridge, stopped in their tracks and looked out on carnage. Donald Philp was kneeling near to the hedge, with a trowel in his hands. Behind him, in the middle of his allotment, lay Arnie in a crater of minced rustic bean canes. Arnie had flown through the hedge in front of Philp, passed over his head and demolished his bean patch. Had he been standing up, he would undoubtedly have been horrifically killed. The old man was, and was most certainly entitled to be, in shock.

"Bloody hell, Philp, you're a lucky man to be alive," announced Bullock loudly.

Philp stared at him glassily, unable to comprehend what had just occurred.

De'Ath arrived shaking and caked in malodorous filth and boiled rice. "Oh my God Almighty. Mr. Philp are you alright?!"

"He's untouched!!" answered Bullock. "I dread to think what would have happened if he'd been stood up!" He put his hand on Philp's shoulder. Philp started. "Why," chuckled Bullock, "we'd have been digging you in for compost now, old lad. Eh?"

Philp still could not speak. Perhaps these two were really trying to kill him. "Come on over to your shed Mr. Philp, I'll make you a nice strong cup of tea." De'Ath helped the old man away; who was still clutching his trowel tightly.

"Aye, make me one an all Tom, I think we've all had a bit of a shock. I shall bloody kill Tony when I get hold of him!"

They all sat in Philp's shed with mugs of tea. Philp had recovered from a severe bout of shaking and had an old blanket draped on his shoulders. Bullock shook his head.

"I shall bloody kill Tony when I get hold of him. Oh, GettaTool will pay for the damage, Mr. Philp! And none of them old sticks, neither, nice new bamboo canes, and good expensive plastic netting. Can't afford that on a state pension old lad, eh? Now then, Mr. Philp, would you like a nice ride home in the Rover? Can't have you on your bike after a shock like that."

Philp looked at Bullock askance. What next, he thought, shoved from the back seat of a moving car? "No, no thanks," he stammered, "I'll be fine, fine thank you. Er, just, erm, move that, er, thing, and I'll be back doing the planting."

"Now, Mr. Philp, there's plenty of time for that, let's run you home, perhaps a quick check-up at the hospital?" protested De'Ath.

"No, really, the patch will be best..." said Philp, opening the door. Bullock slapped him on the back, making him jump again.

"Aye that's the gardening spirit, Philp, the healing of the land and all that. Come on Thomas, let's do as the man says and get that bloody death trap off his patch."

"Aye, but there's always a funny side, Thomas. You should have seen yourself being hauled along in the shite. Now we must have a video camera just in case in future. That would have bloody cleaned up on Beadle. That and Swamp Thing, oh dear, we'd have been famous!"

It was the following day. Bullock and De'Ath were slowly digging their patch with forks. The ooze seemed to have disappeared. "Tony is a lucky man. Do you know if he wasn't my son-in-law, I'd bloody sue him. Oh, morning, Mr. Philp, feeling better are we?"

Philp was arriving on his bicycle, looking very pale. He waved meekly. Bullock leaned over to De'Ath. "Wait 'til he sees what we've done," he whispered with a grin. The pair followed him onto his patch. They had made a cockeyed attempt to repair his bean patch, his old hazel wands having been replaced by brand new bamboo canes. New seedlings had been rather carelessly planted around the bomb crater. Philp surveyed the scene balefully.

"Eh, and that's not all!" announced Bullock from the footbridge. "We thought we'd mark the spot of your lucky escape with a monument." Bullock, feeling a certain triumph in having made his considered amends for a near-catastrophe, led Philp to his lettuce patch. There, in the middle, surrounded by poorly and prematurely pricked out lettuce seedlings, was a garden gnome. Philp had a deep loathing of garden gnomes, they always aroused his instant anger. This was an unusual one, he thought, as he bent to examine it, his blood pressure rising. The clay figure was bent in genuflection in what appeared to be a revelatory expression of worship. Both Ron and Tom burst out laughing again when they saw it, for the fifth time that day.

"Aye, he'd landed a fish when we bought him, y'see Mr. Philp" chuckled Bullock. "I broke his rod and fish off. Offering thanks to the Lord now, eh!!"

"Hahaha. Heeheehee. Said the praying gnome," said De'Ath, stupidly.

Philp walked quietly and resolutely into his lettuce patch, not bothering to avoid the seedlings, as he knew they would have to be re-planted. He picked up the gnome, and rising, marched stiffly towards Bullock until he was jaw to jaw with him. Bullock's grin had frozen on his face.

"Feck off me patch now, or I'll shove this up your arse and put a pitchfork up your mate's. Interfere with me or my garden again, and I'll have you in court." He slammed the gnome into Bullock's hands in fury, and stalked off in the direction of his shed. The shed door slammed shut, and a bolt was drawn across on the inside.

Bullock was genuinely shocked. "The ungrateful old git." He stared disbelievingly at at the praying gnome, for which he had expected great praise.

"I hope it wasn't my David Bowie joke that upset him. You know Ron, the Laughing Gnome. One of my favourites that."

"No, I'm sure it wasn't that, Thomas. Probably just still shocked. He'll come and apologise when he's calmed."

Philp peered angrily through one of his shed windows. De'Ath suspected that he was sharpening the prongs of his pitchfork. "Well, he doesn't look very apologetic yet. I suggest an honourable retreat, Ronald."

"Yes, wars have never hurt anybody except the people who die, as Dali said."

The pair scuttled hastily off Philp's patch and over the footbridge. Bullock placed the gnome ruefully on the Shed window ledge. He looked at it lovingly and followed De'Ath inside, gurgling once again with laughter.

- CHAPTER TWO -

Spring

It was a beautiful day in April on Oldside Allotment, and several gardeners were busy in shirtsleeves. Ron and Tom's allotment possessed some burgeoning greenery, but on closer inspection, the emerging vegetables were ragged and juvenile compared to the already bounteous progress on surrounding land. Many of their seedlings were choked by weeds. Despite the warmth, De'Ath and Bullock were holed up in the Shed.

Peering through frowns and pipe fumes, the pair intently studied piles of gardening magazines and books. They had become slowly convinced that nature's chaos and treachery had to be overcome by the wiles and science of men. Bullock's faith in organic gardening was over, De'Ath's was wavering.

"Well, you fight fire with fire. If that auld bugger douses his patch to kill the weeds, and chases the pests off to our patch, we'll have to respond." Bullock was pressing the case for the policy of chemical attack on the weeds, in animated fashion.

De'Ath frowned. "I've never seen Mr. Philp apply any weedkiller or anything like that. He did say to me once that all you needed for a healthy garden was well-rotted manure and a sharp hoe."

"Well, you're not going to believe that old country story, are you? The man's a hypocrite. Why, I saw him the other day with an old pair of bellows gassing his seeds!!"

In fact, Philp was a resolutely organic gardener and had been so all his life. Bullock had seen him with an ancient humidifier, spraying seedlings with water vapour in their cold frames. He had been known to apply an occasional very localised chemical treatment, but through experience, he had learned to grow certain plants together. He encouraged nature on the plot.

"No, Tom, you have to fight fire, with fire," continued Bullock insistently, "can you only imagine how long it would take us to hoe all those bloody weeds out? This is the tool we need, Tommy boy!" Bullock leaned over, jabbing a podgy finger at a full page advertisement for obscure technical gardening equipment.

"A flamethrower?!" exclaimed De'Ath, part in surprise and part in wonder.

"Eh, up, lad, ah knew you'd like it!" chuckled Bullock, re-lighting his pipe.

De'Ath peered at the adveriement, which featured a smiling, check-shirted mid-West American assaulting a hedgerow with a military-looking weapon. He read aloud, as Bullock nodded sagely. "'Though flaming technology has been around since the 1940s, home gardeners have expressed renewed interest in these weed-fighting tools. Flamers are portable gas torches that produce intense heat, about 2,000 dgrees Fahrenheit. When you pass the flame over and around weeds, it quickly boils the water in the plants' cells, causing them to burst. Once the heat destroys any section of a weed's stem, for instance, water and nutrients cannot reach the leaves, and the top part of the weed dies.' Seems reasonable."

Bullock went outside, returning with a handful of goose grass and dock. He resumed his seat, and applied his lighter to the weeds, which duly crackled and blackened. "There you are, *Quod est Demonstratum*, Thomas."

"Ah, effective but dangerous, Ron. Listen to this. 'Never use flame torches around any dry, brown, or otherwise flammable material. Personal safety is another issue. These portable torches use pressurized tanks of propane and, if handled carelessly, can be hazardous. When operated properly, however, flamers are easy-to-use, safe, and timesaving gardening tools.'"

"Well, there you are. Those warnings are not for us, Tom, they are for Americans," said Bullock contemptuously.

De'Ath continued to read. "90 dollars for a flamer. Flamers are long metal tubes that carry gas to the flaming tip. Also includes an extension hose and gas regulator. The propane cylinder is sold separately."

"And who do you think has just ordered one?" interjected Bullock, triumphantly.

"Oh no, not GettaTool again?" groaned De'Ath.

"Nay, nay lad, me! Us! I've bought one off t'internet. Should be here tomorrow. Oh, we'll 'ave a bit of fun *and* torch them weeds! It'll run off Wendy's barbecue cylinder, she said I could borrow it."

"Well, shopping on the internet. I must say, Ron, you are at the forefront of technology, in every way. Tomorrow? Do you really think it will be here?"

"That's what they promised, Tommy. But I must say, I'd doubt it."

Therefore it came as some surprise to Bullock, still in bed at ten o' clock the next morning, to have Bella bellow up the stairs, "Ronny, parcel!"

Bullock had always resented the early start that his career as a sales account manager had usually entailed, and vowed upon his retirement to turn everyday into a weekend lie-in. He was well on the way to succeeding, to the fury of Bella, who was rising earlier and earlier. "I can't do the beds till noon, Dot," she complained, "Tom lies there reading 'The Telegraph'!"

Bullock came downstairs in his stripy pyjamas, to sign for a large Federal Express parcel, the many layers of which he began to unwrap on the kitchen table. "Make us another cuppa, love?"

"What the devil have you got there, Ron Bullock?" replied Bella, putting on the electric kettle, and washing out an old brown tea pot.

"This, my dear Mrs. Bullock, is the Weed Nemesis. Trademark. And it is going to blow all the sonofabitch weeds on my goddam allotment to hell," he replied in a very bad American accent. Bullock pieced together assorted tubes, nozzles and hoses. Assembled, the Weed Nemesis looked a most impressive weapon.

By the time Bella turned around with steaming milky tea with two sugars in a Barnsley Football Club mug with a bulldog on it, Bullock had removed his pyjama top to reveal a string vest, and he was pointing the flamethrower in Bella's direction. He had one of Bella's unlit Embassies dangling from his mouth. "Welcome to the pardy, pal" he drawled. It wasn't a bad Bruce Willis impersonation, given that Bullock's resemblance to him was scant.

The cackling Bella caught him straight in the forehead with a wet J-Cloth, at which Bullock feigned a clumsy death-fall that resulted in him upturning the bullet bin and landing on Baskerville, who was as usual, sleeping in his basket. The rudely awakened dog, who had been dreaming of squirrel-catching, regarded his master's dripping, reddened, creased and laughter-gasping face with long-suffering disdain. "I ought to bite your stupid strawberry nose for that" he thought. "But I won't. Never bite the hand that feeds, Basker." And the wise old dog licked Bullock's face, with doggy affection. And went back to sleep.

By mid afternoon, the flamethrower was ready for action. Wendy's barbecue cylinder was hitched to the Weed Nemesis, via a series of bolts and plumber's tape. Bullock had decided to continue his Bruce Willis charade and, encouraged by the unseasonal warmth and dryness of that April afternoon, wore a white vest top, a pair of safety goggles and army pants stuffed into Wellington boots. By contrast, De'Ath wore his Barbour and a worried expression.

"Rrrrrrright, fire 'er up, Tommy, let's razzle and frazzle!!" De'Ath turned on the cylinder, Bullock tripped an ignition switch, and an impressive fork of blue flame shot forth from the nozzle. "He-hey!" shouted Bullock, "it bloody well works! Would you bloomin' believe it?"

Bullock set about frying weeds with alarming vigour. De'Ath trailed behind him, hauling the large cylinder as the hose extended. Within a half hour, about a quarter of the allotment was charred and blackened. Both men were hot and very pleased. Bullock turned a dial on the flamethrower, and laid it down. He removed his goggles and wiped his sweating brow with a freckly arm.

"That is a bloody marvel, that is. Where's that wasps nest that keeps bothering us. Let's have it." Having located the nest in a hollow tree near the hedgerow, the nest and all its sleepy inhabitants were summarily incinerated. Bullock laughed maniacally as he gave the sign to De'Ath to turn off the gas. "Wasps annihilated, captain. All turned off, Tom? Gut, lets 'ave a brew."

Over tea, the two exchanged amazement at how well things were going. "I can't understand why these are not in more common use, Tom. So effective."

"And so much more ecological than herbicides, Ron. All this lot will just rot in. Right, my turn I reckon. I'll start at the top of my old patch." De'Ath began hauling the Weed Nemesis and the cylinder towards his old shed, the Orange Box, and Bullock hurried to assist.

"OK, Tommy, ready to go. Ground Control to Major Tom."

De'Ath donned the safety goggles. "Take your protein pill and put your helmet on! 3,2,1…Check ignition, and may God's love be with you!" he sang to himself. De'Ath was very fond of early David Bowie. Somewhere, he had a faded "Space Oddity" T-shirt that he used to wear. He wondered where it was. This thought distracted him, at a moment he should not have been distracted. A few vital seconds later, he switched the ignition of the Weed Nemesis, and looked in vain for the fine fork of blue flame to emerge. Instead, there was a roaring sound behind him. Bullock and De'Ath turned to see flames pouring from the top of the barbecue cylinder, which resembled a gigantic blowtorch. De'Ath threw down the Weed Nemesis in panic and began involuntarily to jump up and down, like John Cleese at the end of his tether.

"Tommy, run for cover!" shouted Bullock "the bloody cylinder might blow!!" They ran to the other side of the allotment. Bullock dived rather unnecessarily into the long grass, perhaps still in Bruce Willis mode. Flames were gushing into the walls of the Orange Box, which was already becoming black and charred. "That shed is Harry History!" bellowed Bullock, rising to his knees.

"Fire brigade, Ron?!" panted De'Ath.

Suddenly, they were elbowed aside. Philp marched between them. "Stand back you useless beggars".

Philp, wearing a pair of asbestos gloves, and carrying a fire extinguisher, calmly approached the gas cylinder and turned it off. The blue flames stopped, but the Orange Box was roaring with flame, the roofing sheets dripping gobs of boiling tar and the window panes cracking with the heat. Philp turned on the extinguisher and began playing it onto the burning shed.

"Used to be in the fire service!" he shouted.

Bullock approached, and to the annoyance of Philp, attempted to direct his fire-fighting. "That's it, Philp, get some over this side, that's a lad!"

"Bugger off out of the way, Bollock!" shouted Philp, "or I'll put you out!"

De'Ath hopped around the conflagration ineffectually.

"Get out of the way, Death, you're too near the flames!"

shouted Philp, in exasperation.

Fifteen minutes later, the fire was out, but the Orange Box was reduced to a charred and sodden shell. All three sat on the ground next to it. "Well done, Philp, fancy having an extinguisher in your shed. Talk about prepared!" congratulated Bullock.

"Well you never know," replied a sooty and gasping Philp, "you never know when a bonfire or gas stove can get out of hand. But what the bloody hell was that contraption?!"

The Weed Nemesis lay charred and twisted, like an exploded Dalek.

"That were a bloody good tool, that were!" announced Bullock, shaking his head and the folds of his neck. "Until dreamboat here forgot to ignite t'gas. I think we had what they call a backdraft. Too much gas in t' hose, late ignition, buusch, must have blown a hole in the hose."

"Yes, I am sorry, Ron. It was my fault."

"Well, you've paid the price with your own shed, Death." said Philp sternly. "And I have to say, I was happy to see the bloody thing burn, personally. That wasn't an allotment shed, that was a rotten suburban summerhouse! Bet you got it from BettaGardens?" All three laughed at this, and De'Ath nodded in some shame, that indeed, he had.

"And why on Earth did you paint it orange, man?" asked Philp, "I remember thinking, what is that bloke doing painting his shed orange?"

"Oh, it wasn't paint," returned De'Ath, "that was Cu-Protect, a combined woodstain and wood preservative. 'Autumn Hues', I believe."

"'Orrible," spat Philp. "At least creosote soaks in and protects the wood. That stuff makes wood look... well, plastic. And the colours...cherry plastic, orange plastic, chocolate plastic..."

"Christ, what's that singeing smell?" interrupted Bullock, "it smells like someone's hair is on fire."

"DAAAAHHH! Me beards a-fire!!" yelled De'Ath, leaping to his feet. His beard was glowing gently at the ends.

Philp, with a gleam in his eye, reached out for his extinguisher. In a moment, De'Ath's head was no longer smouldering, but a mass of foam, much to the amusement of Bullock, who rolled around the floor gasping with laughter.

It was May Day, the hawthorn hedges were white with flower. Bullock and De'Ath were hoeing weeds, the former very resentfully. Bullock was puffing and sweating with a Dutch hoe, whilst De'Ath was attempting to push a cog-wheel contraption he had bought to try to make amends for his ruination of the Nemesis. Bullock was not impressed with it.

"Yer mekin' little headway, tha' knows! It's getting caught on these big clods. What did you call it again?"

De'Ath stopped for a moment, equally over-heated, and he loosened the cravat at his neck, and mopped his brow. "It's a Wolf soil miller, Ron. It's supposed to break down the soil and cut down the weeds in one motion. But you're right, I think it's really for finer soils, or tilth, as they say."

"Tilth? Who says? You've made it up." Bullock's mood was becoming blacker.

"Tilth, Ron? A crumbly soil. Like Mr. Philp's."

"Bloody Weed Nemesis would have had this done in an hour," muttered Bullock to himself, resuming his toil.

De'Ath, with a slightly trimmed beard following his singeing, was oblivious to Bullock's bad mood. "I was reading, Ron, that there are biological control methods available."

"Oh aye?" returned Bullock distractedly.

"Yes, it says that you buy these packets of dried tiny worms, they call them nematodes, mix 'em up in water, pour em on your patch, and they attack the slugs, and nothing else."

Bullock was still imagining frying weeds.

"Yes, they carry germs into the slug, which kill 'em off."

At this, Bullock put down his hoe again. "Germs?!!! Good

God man, you mean biological weapons, what do you think we are, bloody Iraqis? Anyhow it sounds too slow, Thomas. We need something fast to get those slugs. I just cannot believe how many there are. You know what I think don't you?"

De'Ath also stopped his ineffectual trundling with the soil miller.

"What I suspect, Tom, is that Philp is throwing his vermin into our patch. I mean, there's hardly any slug or snail damage on his plot. Ours is acrawl with 'em. Bella is getting fed up with me nicking the salt off her all the time. And it's not just the slugs, eh. Flies, weeds, every pest you can name. No wonder this organic gardening malarkey isn't taking off."

"Yes Ron, it does look as though we will have to resort to the chemicals. Just this season to get us going."

"Aye, come on, lad, let's get down to Mr. Tilletson and see what he's got."

Tom and Ron put the tools in the Shed, closed the door and carefully locked it with a combination padlock. As they tramped towards the lane, Bullock grimaced at a huge juicy slug moving among their beetroot seedlings. He picked it up, inspected it for a second, and flung it high into the air over the hedge towards Philp's plot.

Philp was hunched over his own onion hoe in shirtsleeves. The slug landed squarely on his back with a squelch, causing him to shriek and leap upwards. Mr Philp's nerves had been badly affected by recent events on the allotment. "What the hell was that?" he enquired of himself in a shaky voice, straightening his back. The slug rolled off his shirt to his feet. "Throwing bloody slugs at me now are they? And what shall we do about that, Donald? We'll take this little feller back where he came from, that's what. And give 'em a piece of your mind, too! I ruddy will."

Crossing the footbridge over the brook, he looked out on his neighbours' patch. They had roughly dug the ground over, but Philp felt a tinge of pity for the sorry efforts they had made in sowing and weed control.

"These two just haven't a clue, they've got green fingers like lumberjacks," Philp told the slug, which was hoping to feel the wet earth beneath its belly again. "No, you'll have to come with me. It's my duty to help these blokes get started, even if they do throw heavy machinery and God's creatures at me. Off you go."

He lobbed the slug into the brook, where it was washed downstream. The animal's primitive nervous system indicated that things were not going well as it tumbled along. "Too wet" it thought. But its slow drowning and eventual ingestion by a swarm of tadpoles represented an ecologically honourable death. Perhaps not as good as that of its parent, who had fallen in a beer trap, but preferable to the chemical holocaust which was about to befall the rest of its kind occupying Bullock and De'Aths allotment.

A nursery like Tilletson's was becoming a rarity in England. Family-owned, it grew much of its own stock and was run by qualified nurserymen. Its tiny shop-front outlet was in a back street in town, but the gardening cogniscenti knew that they could buy their plant stock, chemicals and even tools at trade prices over a strong mug of tea with floating compost from the nursey itself. The nursery occupied several acres of suburban Oldside. Its huge greenhouses were pre-war, one heated by a heaving and struggling coal boiler. Venerable oaks and horse chestnuts lined the site where tawny owls nested and hunted the mice and rats that pillaged the potting sheds by night. It was dirty, it was friendly, it was rugged. And it was going out of business.

Proprietor Percy Tilletson greeted Ron and Tom heartily as they clambered out of Ron's brown Rover, both wearing beany hats sporting the logo 'Tilletson's Grow Better Gardeners'. De'Ath thought Tilletson seemed a little weary, but Bullock did not notice.

"Lovely to see you gentlemen on such a fine morning." Percy Tilletson was a gentleman and a botanical scholar. He gave true meaning to the word 'debonair'. He wore a country check shirt from Jermyn Street, a discreet brown tartan tie from a Scottish woollen mill, a green moleskin waistcoat, and worn, hand-made corduroy trousers. His boots were hob-nailed and highly polished, his Barbour coat freshly waxed. His large, hooked nose and melodious, rich, dark voice were his extraordinary features. And his handshake. Tilletson came from a part of England's heritage where this human contact was important. It wasn't a perfunctory ritual, and it was nothing to do with the 'funny handshake' brigade. It was a way of communicating and a means of ascertaining. Coupled with his eye contact, Percy Tilletson had quite consciously developed his handshake to a form of language.

Bullock appreciated a man with a good handshake, and heaving himself out of the car, he offered his own podgy paw. Bullock was always surprised at how work-calloused Tilletson's right palm was, like leather; a boss who did his own digging. Tilletson knew that he could convey warmth, sympathy, humour, sadness and steely warning through his palm. He knew the power of intentionality, of transmitting purpose. But his ability to do this was tempered by the sensitivity of the other to receive. His second wife never forgot her introduction to Tilletson; his firm enveloping of her hand had sent an electric warmth which spread through her body, and settled in a pool just below her navel. Jaded men arriving at the nursery were energised by his grasp.

For Bullock though, handshaking was simply a test of manhood, and for him, he who gripped hardest and shook most hearty was the better man. A bit like arm wrestling, but briefer. Tilletson didn't mind his hand being gripped and shaken like a poisonous snake, as he appreciated Bullock's heartiness, which made him smile. He was less enthusiastic about receiving De'Ath's bony, clammy hand.

When Bullock had introduced himself to De'Ath on the allotment several months ago with a proferred hand, the Yorkshireman was not impressed. "Handshake like a wet lettuce. Can't be getting on with a bloke like that," he had thought to himself alone in his Shed. Fortunately, De'Ath's redeeming qualities proved to make up for his limp handshake. De'Ath himself had just never got handshakes. He had no notion of any contained meaning. He found it, in general, pointless and perhaps containing just a little more intimacy than was strictly required in a greeting, especially between men.

Tilletson had once lightly squeezed the small gloved hand of the Queen. How terrible, he had thought, to be a professional meeter-and-greeter, even a royal one. Her hand was devoid of feeling, her eye contact fleeting and disinterested. It was difficult to make eye contact with De'Ath at all. A keen fisherman, in holding De'Aths hand, Tilletson was always put in mind of a three-quarter pound bream, the limpest and slimiest of all freshwater fish. He was far too much a gentleman to do it, but he really did feel like wiping his hand on his cords after releasing De'Ath's. But he had also come to like this wispy-bearded fellow and he welcomed them both to a potting shed with an ancient manual till, a kettle and a ceramic sink full of dirty mugs. He made them all tea himself, and they sat outside on a bench, where Tilletson's two lurcher dogs were lying obediently. "Now then, Mr Bullock, Mr. De'Ath, do we owe the pleasure of your visit to a specific reason this fine day?"

"Well, Mr. Tilletson, we've had a go at this organic gardening on our allotment, y'know. We've give it a gut go. But we think we need a little bit of help from old Mr. Mendeleev."

"Mr. Mendeleev?" asked Tilletson, slightly taken aback.

"Y'know, him who invented t'Periodic Table of

Elements. T'father of chemistry." Bullock grinned, pleased with his rhetoric.

"Phew, that's a relief, I thought you were on about that German bastard who experimented on people at Auschwitz! I don't think he ever messed about with plant genetics though!"

De'Ath looked into the distance. "Ah, yes, Josef Mengele, you mean. Contender for the most evil man of all time, I should say..."

"Oh, 'ell Mengele, no, we don't want his bloody help thanks very much!" spluttered Bullock.

"I'm sorry, I still can't quite forgive the Germans, you know." Tilletson rejoined. "I occasionally have nightmares about how it would have been if things would have been, you know, if we hadn't have done so well in the Battle of Britain, if we hadn't fought so bloody well, and worked so hard at home. If we had just capitulated like the French, and OK, if the Yanks hadn't got involved..."

"We'd 'ave fought even harder on our own soil, Mr. Tilletson. We'd 'ave fought em to the death, every last British man and woman," scowled Bullock.

De'Ath had sprung up from the bench, agitated and animated, and grabbed a fork lying in a nearby wheelbarrow. "That's what my old mum had ready for them...evil swine, try knocking on our door then, and see what for!!"

Bullock and Tilletson could not help laughing at his comic pose. "Oh, eck, Thomas you look like Corporal Jones!! They don't like it up 'em, sir!!" gasped Bullock.

Tilletson got to his feet chuckling in baritone and gently escorted De'Ath back to a seated position; he did seem to have become over-excited.

"I know what you mean Mr. Tilletson," said De'Ath, "I can't forgive them either." His hand shaking a little, he took a sip of tea, which seemed to calm him down. He smiled his rather beautiful smile, and began to sing. "Who do you think you are kidding, Mr.Hitler…"

Tilletson and Bullock joined in enthusiastically, "…if you think we're on the run. We are the boys who will stop your little game, we are the boys who will make you think again!!" The men were in such good voice, swinging their fists in time with their song, that one of the nurserymen emerging from a greenhouse fifty yards away was able to join loudly in with the last line "…IF YOU THINK OLD ENGLAND'S DONE!!!"

The song ended with much laughter and back-slapping. "Bill," called Tilletson, "have you met Mr. De'Ath and Mr. Bullock? They have taken a couple of plots at Oldside allotment, and need some advice on pesticides and so on. Now, gentlemen, I must leave you, I have an appointment in town. I did enjoy our little sing-song, I must say, it's good for chaps to sing, isn't it? Now then, Bill will advise you on whatever you need." Tilletson thought about a farewell handshake, but thought of a bream and a vice, and decided on a salute. Receiving dutiful salutes from all three, he turned, snapped his fingers, and the lurchers were at once leaping into the open boot of his muddy Volvo.

"Now, then, what sort of chemicals do you need?" asked Bill, a genial heavyweight in a tartan workman's shirt. "Are we fertilizing or pestisising?"

"What we want, Bill," said Bullock, looking the man seriously in the eye, "is the full artillery. You see, it has set us back this organic gardening. We want t'weeds to be gone, and we don't want all t'slugs and flies we seem to 'attract'."

"Right, right," said Bill, stroking his chin, "well, come with me, we'll fix you up with some general herbicide and some insecticide. Some slug pellets as well."

Bill gave a brief tour of the storeroom, and left them with a trolley. "Just give me a shout if you want any more help" he called as he went back to the greenhouse.

De'Ath and Bullock were left to mutter conspiratorially in the gloom of a dusty 40 Watt bulb. "OK Thomas, we're agreed. No prisoners."

"Belt and braces, Ron; prevention is better than cure."

They loaded up the entire aged wooden trolley to buckling point with boxes, sacks, canisters, drums, shakers, sprays and bottles. And a rubber model of a sparrowhawk, intended to deter pigeons. As they struggled to heave the trolley round, De'Ath was alarmed by a figure behind them, who had evidently been watching them for some while.

"Sorry to startle you, zurs," the figure grunted from the shadows, "I was just wonderin' if you needed any help, like?" A very old man less than five feet tall, with few teeth and a huge scarlet face, was gaping disconcertingly.

"Er…we're about right, thanks, olt chap," offered Bullock backing away slightly, taken aback by the man's appearance. He didn't think he'd ever seen a face quite as ugly, anywhere. The word 'monstrous' leapt into his head. The old man was not at all disconcerted by the evident alarm at his appearance. He was far too used to it. He shuffled forward into the dim light of the bulb, prodding at the chemical assortment. "Blimey, you fellers have got some problems by the look of this lot?!"

"Aye, we've an infestation olt lad. Sheer infestation. We don't like using chemicals of course, but needs must in this instance, needs must."

The ancient nurseryman nodded his head in vigorous agreement. "Aye, needs must, zurs, needs must. Mind you..." he announced theatrically, with a wink which involved the contortion of the whole left side of his face, "piss-poor these chemicals nowadays."

"Are you saying these won't do the job?" inquired De'Ath sceptically, pointing at the arsenal on the trolley.

"Nononononono, zurs, allus I'm saying is the chemicals aren't as good as they *was*." He looked around, conspiratorially. He lowered his voice slightly. "Now you takes yer creosote for example. Now I remember the times when if you got a drop of that in your eye, you was blinded for days. Blinded for days you was! Why now, you could wash in the stuff!! By God, that didn't just kill pests; it kept 'em away. Y'see gents..." He now leaned closer and mimicked dipping something in a barrel, "...an old sock or two dipped in creosote, hung around the veg plot, kept 'em away, it did."

Bullock was taken with this idea. He certainly remembered the old creosote on his larch lap fencing and its pungent, persistent and toxic qualities. He could well imagine its propensity to deter pests. "No good now you say, with modern creosote?"

"Oh, no zur, waste of time. Bloody invironmintilists, y'see. All the decent stuff banned, restricted or watered down."

"It is as you say, the environmental movement causes as many problems as it solves. I would like to get my hands on some of those decent chemicals."

This was clearly the cue that the old man had awaited. He timed his pause and wore his conspiratorial air to perfection. "I can see you lads are my sort. I've seen you in here a lot. If you can keep it secret, I can get you the good stuff. None of these Sunday chemicals."

De'Ath looked contemptuously at their trolley. "Sunday chemicals. Like at BettaGardens."

All three looked scornful at the mention of the gardening emporium on the edge of town.

"What are we talking about here, nothing too illegal I hope?" asked Bullock.

"Well, let's see now. I can get you some decent creosote I stockpiled in me shed. Don't need much, see. A pint or two a year. Now, I've a farmer mate can sell you some permethrin, and decent lindane; not banned, gents, just restricted use to them as knows; and I've got me own supplier of the proper stuff...."

The whistling of the Dad's Army theme tune heralded Bill's return. "Blimey, you've got a long supply there, gents. Cliff! I didn't see you there. Not holding these two gentlemen up I 'ope?"

The little ogre opened his mouth to reply, but was beaten by Bullock. "Not at all, not at all, Bill. The old feller was giving us a bit of gardening lore, you know, very interesting too."

"Oh aye? Cliff, can you sort this lot out at the till? I've got to get some more compost to the girls pricking out."

"No problem at all, Bill, you get on your way. Can't have Joyce and Gwen heaving bags of compost about."

All three pushed the creaking trolley towards the yard. "Now, as I was saying, the proper stuff. DDT..."

De'Ath stopped pushing the trolley, and it stopped dead. "DDT, that was banned years ago!!"

"Not so hasty, Thomas, hear the man out. I was reading in The Telegraph just the other day how DDT spraying saves millions of lives from malaria."

"That's right, mate. Kills orf the morsquito like it kills orf every other bloomin' garden pest. Can't be beat. Swears by it, I do, and I been a village Show Master eight times for proof."

Bullock now recognized the man from a photograph he had seen in the village hall, with a silver cup. He had remarked then what an appallingly ugly fellow that was. "And if we were to be interested in purchasing from you a can or two?"

"Well if you was to give me fifty quid I could bring you enough for a trial spraying which should last the summer. All hush course. If you was to blab, I'd know nowt."

"What d'y think, Watson, worth a shot, eh?"

"I'm doing nothing illegal, Tom, if were caught using DDT the Parish Council would throw us off. And I'd be thrown off the Parish Council, and well, disgrace all round."

"Steady on, old lad," intervened the ancient. "All us gardeners use it! If anybody asks where you got such a good bug killer you tell 'em you found it in your shed marked "insecticide". That's what I'd do."

"Sounds plausible. Well I'm game for anything once. If anything happens, the responsibility shall be mine, Thomas," said Bullock, with a stubborn air.

"I'm having none of that, Ron. You go down, we both go down. Let's give it a go."

"Right then, that's settled. Mr. ...?"

"Dredge."

"Mr. Dredge, here's our allotment address; let me draw you a little map. Bring us some creosote and, er, DDT when you can. It really is most kind of you to share with us your gardening expertise. And confirms to me once again the superiority of Tilletson's over lugubrious enterprises like BettaGardens."

"They're a load of pansy nancy yuppie townie know-nothing arseholes. Couldn't grow watercress on a windersill." The monstrous little man scowled and spat expertly and impressively into the earth. Sometimes, a good spit really is better than a thousand expletives, thought Bullock. De'Ath was thinking the exact same thing, and for some peculiar reason, he felt inclined to a show of male solidarity by spitting himself.

"Couldn't have put it better myself!" De'Ath announced and then spat a large mouthful of white spittle onto his own beard and shirt.

"Rats!" he muttered, embarrassed and quickly busy with his hankerchief.

Bullock attempted to look as though he had not witnessed this self-disgrace, but Dredge had no breeding or manners whatsoever and began pointing at De'Ath and cackling. Bullock felt like cracking Dredge on the head with an imagined silver-handled cane for his impertinence, but settled for bringing the interview to a terse close. "Well, good day, Mr. Dredge, we look forward to your delivery. Come on Tom, let's get this stuff aboard!"

Dredge hobbled, still cackling, back to the nursery, bumping into Bill again. "I hope you have not been trying to flog your chemical arsenal, Cliff. If I catch you doing that you know I'll have to sack you on the spot."

"Oh dear no, Mr. Tibbs. Just offering those gentlemen a few tips on weeding. "Blow your sprays I was saying, just keep the hoe busy." Then that dozy-looking bugger spat on his own self! Oh, dear, priceless, that was, priceless!!" Bill shook his head, unamused and unconvinced, and left to water the summer bedding seedlings. When he was out of sight, Dredge picked up the telephone.

Just as Dredge was making his furtive calls, Percy Tilletson was striding into the warehouse world and piped music of BettaGardens. Past the ranks of garden furniture he strode, past the tea shop and the shelves of fluffy toys; he arrived at the information desk, where a confused-looking lady was inspecting a large pot plant with patches of yellow on its waxy fronds. An anxious young couple were consulting her on its ailment. "Are you watering it?" asked the information lady, hopefully.

Tilletson intervened. "That is a rather lovely Philodendron. May I ask where you keep it?"

"We have a little conservatory, we keep it there," offered the young woman.

Tilletson inspected the leaves carefully. "Well, these plants don't like draughts. And they like humidity."

The woman's husband chipped in. "Yes, it's by the back door. It will get a draught there."

"Well, try moving it out of the draught, and sit it on a moist pebble tray. Give it a spray with tepid water every so often, it will enjoy that."

The couple thanked Tilletson and popped the plant back

in a trolley. "Right, it's a good spray for you," the woman was telling the plant.

"And we'll soon get rid of those nasty spots," her husband added. They trundled it away, like a slightly poorly child in a pram.

"I hope that I didn't steal your thunder, my dear," Tilletson apologized to the information lady, whose name was Brenda.

"No, not at all! Quite the opposite. I don't know a thing about plants."

"Oh, I see," said Tilletson, puzzled. "Well, anyhow, my dear, I have an appointment with Mr. MacMeddler."
At that moment a pin-striped youth swaggered past, shouting into a tiny mobile phone pressed to his ear. "Yeah, well, I don't wanna 'ear that do, I?" he kept repeating. Seeing Tilletson, McMeddlar stopped, continued his monotonous conversation into his mobile at his right ear and advanced his small sweaty left palm to Tilletson.

Tilletson was at a loss. How extraordinary! he thought. Not only is he not greeting me, he is offering his left hand to shake!! He was really baffled at how to respond.

"S'awlright Perce," whined McMeddler, in an irritating faux-London drawl and snapping closed his phone, "I 'aven't wiped me bum with this one!! Ha, aha, aha!"
Tilletson regarded McMeddler's young, unattractive, waxy mirthless face above the huge knot of his shiny purple tie. "Come in, Percy, get us some coffee, Brenda." They entered

McMeddlar's large, modern office.

"S'awlright, innit, Perce?" asked McMeddler rhetorically, running his fat hands over the wall panels, "all mahogany? I insist on a nice office. You know why?" The young executive bared his yellowy rodent teeth in what Tilletson assumed was his smile. He raised an eyebrow slightly in reply. "Cos I spend a lot of time here, mate. Do you know what the secret of my success is?"

Tilletson had not the faintest interest in the secret of McMeddler's putative success.

"Mr. McMeddlar..." he started.

"Please, Perce, call me Marcus," interrupted BettaGardens' store manager, falling into a leather swivel chair and folding his hands behind his coarse, spiky hair. "Take the weight orf yer pins."

Tilletson sat uneasily down and attempted to begin again. "Well, er, Marcus...I thought I'd come over...."

"I put in the hours, mate. That's the secret. I'm here before anyone else. Up at five. Everyday. That's the secret. Up early. Work hard, play hard, that's me."

"Well, I'm an early riser myself," began Tilletson, "I mean, you have to be in the nursery..."

Suddenly McMeddler shot forward from his chair as if bitten by a snake. "That's all very interesting Perce. Very interesting," he said, aggressively nodding his head, "but let's just cut to the chase. Have you reconsidered our offer?"

At that moment a phone trilled. "Don't mind if I get that, Perce?" Without waiting for a response, McMeddler grabbed the phone and began walking round the office. "Andy! How are you, you old wanker? No? No? Did she? Ha, aha, aha! Did she? No? Yeah, nice, one, hang on, I'll just get into my diary." McMeddler winked at Tilletson as he shifted and clicked at a computer mouse. Tilletson made no reply. He did not think he had met such a repulsive and charmless creature in all his days. "How about a week Thursday? No? Two weeks Friday? No?! How about never, is never good for you? No, I'm joking, you arsehole! Ha, aha, aha! Listen, call me in a couple of weeks. Yeah. Diamond. Take care mate. Wicked. Yeah, you too."

"Sorry, Perce...ah, Brenda, coffee, thought you'd gone to Brazil to grow it!" The worried-looking woman arrived with a tray of vending machine coffee. "You didn't get a Brazillian whilst you were there, eh? Ha, aha, aha!"

Tilletson took a perfunctory sip from his polystyrene cup as Brenda retreated, wordless and embarrassed. He had decided to make this short. He looked sternly into the narrow eyes of Marcus McMeddler. "I've come by to say that Tilletson's Nurseries is not for sale to Betta Gardens at any price, Mr. McMeddler."

McMeddler nodded petulantly. "Well, I don't mind saying I'm disappointed to hear that, Perce. For your sake. Because I won't be in a position to dig you out of the shit next time. It wont be me, Percy, it will be the liquidator. How much of your life have you got locked into that business? All the real estate, your car? Your home? Gardening is commodified mass market, Percy, it's not niche no more. Businesses like yours are yesterdays chip paper, mate. From what I hear about your books, you wanna cash your chips in whilst they're worth summink." He took a voracious gulp of coffee and continued. Do you know what I know about plants? Nuffink. Do you know what I care about plants? Nuffink. But it don't stop me putting you out of business. Think about it. You get to retire with full honours and plenty of cash in the bank. We'll have to close the shop, but we'll re-develop the nursery. I'll look at taking on every one of your staff for coming to work for us with no wage drop." The phone trilled. "Don't mind if I get that Perce?"

Tilletson had had enough. He rose and walked out of the office. As he drove back to his nursery, a deep depression began to set in. My England is over, he reflected.

It was very early on a mid-May morning, cold, and only just light. De'Ath was in the Shed, beginning to inspect the highly suspicious petrol cans delivered, as arranged, the previous evening by Cliff Dredge. He jumped when there came a knock at the door. He imagined for a moment two uniformed police inspectors arriving to arrest him for illegal possession of hazardous chemicals. To his relief came the voice of Bullock. "Knock, knock."

He remembered their code words. "Who's there?"

"Lettuce."

"Lettuce who?"

"Lettuce in and you'll find out."

Bullock entered with a conspiratorial air. "How many olt socks did yer get, Tommy?"

"Four, Ron as agreed. And you?"

"Aye, four as agreed."

"Right, let's get into these and get going." Bullock produced two protective white suits obtained from GettaTool, complete with elasticated hood, cuffs and ankles. They bumbled around the Shed, bumping into each other, Bullock complaining about the early hour. They also donned rubber gloves, face masks, and goggles. With a peer outside to check that no one was around, they set about their skullduggery. De'Ath began dunking old socks into a bucket of evil smelling brown liquid using clothes tongs. Bullock filled a huge pesticide gun, called RoboCop III, with a funnel from one of the petrol cans marked 'Speshal Brew', in wobbly white letters. The white-suited figures then wandered around for the next half hour, arranging foully dripping socks on bean poles and spraying the ground with deadly insecticide.

Also making an early start that day were Wendy Wakaya and Phillip Ward. As the early commuter train rumbled along the embankment, Phillip peered out of the grimy windows. He had become much more keen of late to wave to Wendy's father, being hopeful of a tale of equal hilarity to tell his workmates. Wendy had become less keen. "You won't see them at this hour," she remarked peevishly from behind her 'Daily Express'. "Dad doesn't get up until ten these days."

"Well who are those blokes then?" responded Phillip with excitement. "Good grief, Wendy. Looks like the decontamination squad have moved in. Must have been dangerous stuff, your father's urine. Either that or there's been a nuclear gardening accident! Bloody hell!" Phillip rose from his seat and peered incredulously. "They've got a bazooka!!"

Bullock and De'Ath were too absorbed by their work to notice the train. "Right, all done?" said Bullock, muffled by his mask.

"Roger one" replied De'Ath, equally muffled, with a thumbs-up sign. They divested themselves of their protective clothing in the Shed, which was piled into a plastic carrier bag for off-site disposal.

"Right, lad, decontaminating showers and a fried breakfast, in that order," grunted Bullock.

"And back here lunchtime, Ron?"

"Aye, sounds good."

By nine o' clock, it was becoming warmer, with a south-westerly breeze. Philp was unhappy with the smell it brought to his nostrils as he arrived at the allotment, but, wrinkling his nose, put it down to the unpredictable emissions from the nearby cement works. But after half an hour of tying in his sweet peas, his eyes began to water. After an hour, he began to cough and wheeze. By eleven o'clock, as he went to his shed for his usual elevenses, his nose and eyes were streaming, and he was sure that he was coming down with a severe cold.

At noon, Ron and Tom returned to the allotment, spruce and decontaminated. Bullock wore a peaked baseball hat with "Head Gardener" embroidered on it. De'Ath, his hair still wet from the shower, prowled around the allotment inspecting the foliage, whilst Bullock, his face pink and shaven, surveyed the scene, hands on hips. "Aye, pongs a bit, but so does bloody manure, eh!" he remarked.

"First victim, Tom," De'Ath called from the hedgerow. "Look at this snail. Dead as a dodo."

Bullock hurried over to inspect the late creature, which was emitting a foaming exudate. "Really?! By God, that's fast acting stuff. Bloody brilliant...aye, look, another one, and these ladybirds are all dead too!!"

"Oh, and just look at this slug, Ron" remarked De'Ath, becoming excited as he picked up a lifeless, disheveled mollusc. "'E's passed on! This slug is no more! 'E's ceased to be! 'E's expired and gone to meet 'is maker! 'E's a stiff! Bereft of life, 'e rests in peace! 'Is metabolic processes are now 'istory! 'E's kicked the bucket, 'e's shuffled off 'is mortal coil, run down the curtain and joined the bleedin' choir invisible!! THIS IS AN EX-SLUG!!"

Both men were of the character able to recite, word for word, many of the Monty Python sketches, and the 'Dead Parrot Sketch' was one of De'Ath's favourites. Once, in a university bar, he had begun reciting the sketch loudly, to the amusement of his geeky chums. A drunken rugby player had lurched over to him and warned him loudly that he would resort to violence if De'Ath continued with his monologue. Having ignored this warning, De'Ath was duly duffed up. Since this time, De'Ath had been rather more circumspect in his selection of occasions for the famous monologue. In Ron, he felt he may have an appreciative audience, as he waved around the unfortunate invertebrate.

He was not wrong, as Bullock doubled up in laughter at the sketch. Indeed, he was able to join in. "Well, I'd better replace it, then. Sorry squire, I've had a look 'round the back of the shop, and er, we're right out of slugs."

"I see. I see, I get the picture," rejoined an overjoyed De'Ath.

"I got a parrot."

"Pray, does it slither?"

"Nnnnot really."

"WELL IT'S HARDLY A BLOODY REPLACEMENT, IS IT?!!???!!?" squawked De'Ath triumphantly at the top of his voice.

At this punchline, both men fell about helpless with laughter, slapping their knees. Philp had padded over the footbridge and was watching the two incredulously. Bullock recovered himself sufficiently to greet the old man, who looked, by contrast with the mirth abroad, as though he had been weeping profusely. "Good morning, Mr. Philp, and a beautiful one it is too!" offered a scarlet Bullock.

"What the hell is that pungent smell?" croaked Philp, "it's gassing me downwind. I can't bloody well work!"

"Well, it's the appliance of science, Mr. Philp. An old standby of mine for bad infestations. You stand to benefit too." Bullock pointed proudly to the line of dripping brown socks.

"Oh Christ, it's creosote. I should have recognized it. I'm only bloody allergic to it. Not as bad these days, mind; I did a fence thirty years ago and broke out in a godawful rash. Me hands swelled up like puddings. Well I'm off home. I dare say the socks will dry out by tomorrow. If you'd garden properly, you don't need stuff like that. Good day to you." Philp hobbled off, snivelling into a hankerchief.

"Yes, er, good day Mr. Philp," De'Ath offered cheerily, then lowered his voice to Bullock.

"Did you hear what he said, Ron? Allergic to the old stuff! He'll be onto us in no time. That is a tragic co-incidence, that is."

Bullock considered the matter, whilst pinching one of the folds of his neck. "You're right, Watson. We must dispose of the evidence before Philp returns on the morrow. You bury the socks, I'll pour the rest of the creosote into that ditch."

Half an hour later, after some Burke and Hare-like sneakery, their deed was done.

It was two days later on the allotment. There was an eerie absence of birdsong and the buzz of pollinating insects. The cabbage white butterflies, formerly in profusion in the copses of nettles between allotments, were not to be seen. Neither the occasional plop of a frog entering the ditch to bask, nor the rustling of a wood mouse in the long grass, were to be heard. De'Ath and Bullock, ensconced in the Shed, were blissfully unaware of the mini ecocatastrophe they had precipitated.

"Every last one of 'em Thomas, every last man jack slug and snail. Organic be beggared; we've done it the old fashioned way. Old Philp would be proud; why I'm sure he'd use the stuff himself if he wasn't allergic to it! Now we can really watch our garden grow, Thomas, 100% pest free."

"Yes, I think I'll go and thin our radishes out today, Ron, I'm in the mood for a good day's work."

"Eh, Tom, what is small, red and whispers?" whispered Bullock.

"A hoarse radish," answered De'Ath confidently.

"Oh yer bugger. Thought I'd get y'with that one. Well, I'll leave it to you, lad, I'm taking Bella out to see Wendy and Ranatunga this afternoon. Fijian lad you know. Nice fella, arms like tree trunks. Bella can't stand him, but she manages to hide it. He likes me though, I can tell. Just sits and smiles at whatever I say. Nice fella."

"Not many Fijians in Oldside, Ron. What is he, a rugger player or something?"

"No, he's a chef apparently. Bloody awful if you ask me though. Insists on the native food every time we go round. Gut ache for days, but you can't be rude, eh? Well, have a good day old son, I'll see thee."

De'Ath spent a peaceful morning on the allotment, thinning and weeding. As the sun gently warmed his back, he fell into a meditative world no Benedictine monk could rival. He was in what Dot called 'his own little world'. Within his trance, he was unaware of Philp wobbling down the allotment path on his bike.

"Death, you Death, yes, that's your name isn't it?!" Philp yelled, dismounting clumsily.

At the bleary edge of his vision, De'Ath saw Philp moving towards him. "Mr. Philp, lovely day...Good Lord, what on earth?" De'Ath was able to ascertain, during Philp's staggering approach, that all was not well. Philp's face and hands were disfigured by a hideous rash. De'Ath instinctively backed away, and started to move towards the Shed.

"Oh no you don't." Philp grabbed De'Ath's sleeve, with a grotesquely swollen hand. "You've got some, haven't you?! I've been in bed for two days. Where did you get it?"

De'Ath stood open-mouthed, never before having been man-handled by such a crazed monster.

"Speak up, man or I'm going searching in your Shed."

"You needn't bother, Mr. Philp. After you saw us the other day, we decided not to use any more creosote. We got rid of it, just in case you, er, reacted."

"Reacted? I look like the bloody Elephant Man!! Where did you get that creosote from, Death?" At this point, Philp actually grabbed De' Ath's neck and began shaking him. "Where!?"

De'Ath considered his position, whilst being shaken by the neck. It was not, he thought, a very happy position to find oneself in. "I, er, didn't buy it, Mr. Bullock did," he blurted.

"Bullock," spat Philp, unhanding the shaken De'Ath. "Right, you've not heard the last of this, I intend to find out where that stuff came from and have it reported. That was not modern creosote, that stuff. I'll get to the bottom of this!" He staggered away, muttering.

At exactly the same time that De'Ath was being throttled mid-allotment, his gardening partner was boring his genial son-in-law Ranatunga Wakaya, with tales of his retail past. They were sitting in a suburban garden, which had been entirely transformed into a Fijian jungle grove. A huge pond containing large ornamental fish was surrounded by palms and creeping foliage. A tape and speaker system delivered a realistic version of a Tahitian dawn chorus. The patio was filled by rush matting. A gas-driven barbecue was grilling enormous shrimps and scallops, and Ranatunga was slowly and methodically peeling mangoes.

"So that's a scallop is it, Rana?" said Bullock, poking a congealed sizzling blob.

"Yes, dad, Queen scallop...do you like?"

"Well, it's a change, int 'it...oh, bloody 'ell, what the hell are they on the barbie, are they still alive?!"

Ranatunga had thrown a handful of squid tentacles on the barbecue range, which curled and almost crawled as they cooked. "No, dad, not alive. Squi'?"

"Squi?"

Rana was used to following up his speech with sign

language and made a very convincing cephalopod by flicking the fingers of his giant hand.

"Oh, squid! Yes, I know. I thought they were like onion rings."

Ranatunga smiled indulgently as he resumed his peeling. Bullock was extremely uncomfortable with the calm silence of the Fijian, which made him gabble.

"Anyway, Rana, this guy walks into a jazz bar with a squid under his arm. The barman goes 'You can't bring that in here.' The bloke goes, 'This squid is a marvel. He can play any musical instrument laid down in front of him! I'll put up fifty quid that says this squid can not only play any musical instrument but he can play it better than you've ever heard it played before. Anyway, this bloke up at the bar goes 'I got fifty quid here says your squid can't play my guitar.' And the man drops the fifty notes on the bar and gives the squid the guitar. The squid looks at the guitar, picks it up, tunes it, and plays a note-perfect version of 'Smoke on the Water' by Jimi Hendrix. The man at the bar applauds. 'Truely amazing,' he goes 'here's your fifty quid, worth every penny.' The feller next to him at the bar goes 'Aye, very good, but I have fifty quid here says your squid can't play my saxaphone'. The squid picks up the sax, and belts out a nice little version of 'What a Wonderful World' by Louie Armstrong. 'Really amazing, here's your fifty pounds worth every penny.'"

Rana nodded and grinned. Bullock was encouraged, and continued. "Anyway, the barman walks behind the bar, opens a door to the back room. Comes back with this old dusty set of bagpipes. 'Let's see him play this, then he says!' So the squid picks up the bagpipes, turns it from side to side, scratches its head, turns it from side to side again, then again. 'Come on,' says the owner of the squid, 'get on and play the damn thing!' The squid looks up and says, 'play it? When I figure out how I get its pyjamas off, I'm gonna mate with it!'"

Bullock laughed a hearty laugh, and Rana joined in. "Oh, 'eck we 'ave a laugh eh, son? It's not football that's the international language, it's humour, eh lad?!"

"That's right, dad, that's right. Now, what are these bag of pipes?"

Bullock was not a man of great patience and had little time for explanation. "Well, that's the whole point of the joke, Rana, surely you've seen bagpipes?" he puffed.

"No."

"Oh, well, it's a Scotiish instrument, with a bag of...oh, never mind."

They both fell silent for a while.

Bullock had memorised at an early age a series of 'Strange Tales', which he used to tell his children. "Now here's summat I'll bet you didn't know, Rana. The surgeon and naturalist Frank Buckland was the author of 'Curiosities Of Natural History' and a gourmet...with a most peculiar palate. He cooked and ate anything that moved, that man. On one occasion he boiled an elephant's trunk, but after several days in the pot it was still too tough to eat, so he settled for elephant's trunk soup. On another occasion friends found him making a huge pie filled with chunks of rhinoceros. When a panther died at London Zoo, Buckland asked the curator to dig it up so that he could make panther chops. Panther chops, imagine that on your barbie, Rana!"

Rana was not sure whether to believe Bullock's story or not. He wondered if it was another joke and stopped peeling to listen intently for a punchline. Bullock had reached that point in a story where he was not certain why he was telling it. He looked at Rana's intense brown-eyed quizzical gaze and decided to battle on. "Anyhow, when he heard of a fire at the giraffe house he was back at t'zoo, excited at the prospect of slabs of roasted giraffe. It was said that he inherited his bizarre taste from his father who, legend has it, ate a portion of Louis XIV's embalmed heart."

Rana was thoroughly confused, and wondered whether this was yet another reference to Bullock's favourite tale of the death of Captain Cook by cannibalism. Wendy and Bella appeared in the grove with a tray containing coconuts with coloured plastic straws poking out of the shells. "Here we are boys," said Bella, "jungle juice is served."

Bullock sipped apprehensively at the coconut milk, which was laced with rum. "He was also involved in a scheme to stock Britain's parks with exotic animals which would breed and then be butchered to feed a growing population."

"Oh, no!" sighed Wendy, "You're not boring my darling with 'Strange Tales'?" She draped an arm protectively over Rana's massive shoulders. "Dad used to tell us these stories every Sunday tea."

"That's right, Wendy. D'you remember? Well, anyway, Rana, Buckland's own home was a haven for small animals, with monkeys by the fire to whom he gave beer every night and port on Sundays. A mongoose and pet rats ran free about the house while a jackass let out a loud laugh every thirty minutes. There was even a South African red river hog which his wife had reared. Can you imagine that house, eh?"

"Why did he give the monkeys beer?" asked Rana, completely lost.

"I don't know," replied Bullock thoughtfully. "To get 'em merry I suppose. And another story about him, I was telling this to Thomas at t'allotment the other day, well..." He was interrupted by a trilling noise.

"Dad, it's for you." With clear relief at the interruption of 'Strange Tales', Wendy handed Bullock a portable phone in the shape of a pineapple.

"Thomas, how on Earth did you find me here?..No, I suppose there aren't many Wakayas in the phone book...oh dear...did he really...oh...oh...no, you did the right thing. Yes. OK, Thomas, we're in a tight spot, but I think I have a plan. Go straight to my house. Remain calm, Watson!"

Bullock handed the pineapple phone back to his daughter. "I'm so sorry love, bit of an emergency at the allotment."

"Oh, Dad, you're not leaving!! The luau is nearly ready!"

"Aye, I've got to sort De'Ath out, he's got himself in a mess.

I'll be back in an hour, love."

"What sort of a mess?" asked Bella, "Is Dot all right?"

"Oh aye, nowt to do with Dot. Just a bit o' bother at t'allotment. Nothing I can't handle, but then, there never was, eh love? Eh 'am sorry about the barbie, though, Rana, I was right looking forward to me panther chops, eh lad!" He whacked Rana on the back. "Now, er, eat up, I'll grab some chips on the way back. Tara!"

Fifteen minutes later, De'Ath and Bullock were sitting in Bullock's lounge, the curtains drawn. A clearly shaken De'Ath was sipping at a large whisky glass. "I'm so sorry to drop you in it, Ron."

"No, you did right son, you bought us time, the crucial ingredient. Watch this for getting us out of this little hole!!" Bullock went into the kitchen and returned with a peg on his nose. He picked up the phone receiver and, removing the hankerchief from his blazer pocket with a flourish, placed it over the telephone mouthpiece and dialled a number.

"Yes, hello Bill. I'm afraid I can't say who this is, but I wish to report that one of your employees is selling banned agricultural chemicals under the counter. Yes, that's right, Mr. Dredge. I see. Yes, cheap timber treatments and the like. Lethal stuff. I've come out in a rash since stupidly buying some. It brings down the name of Tilletson's. Yes. Well I'll consider the matter closed, in that case. I will continue to shop at your fine establishment. Yes. Yes. Good day to you." He replaced the receiver chortling. "There we go! Dredge summarily dismissed. Justice done and seen to be done, Thomas."

De'Ath slumped with shame. "You shopped him, Ron. To save our skin."

But Bullock was an expert in history re-writes. "Shopped? The man is a public nuisance! Always thought he was the bad apple at Tilletson's."

"He'll know it was us, Thomas, got him sacked. He'll be after us."

"If that old buzzard wants trouble from us, he'll get a bloody nose and no mistake. Right, I'm off back to Fiji. P'raps they'll have finished that rubbish they cook. Do you know what's for pudding? Durians. Smell like rotting flesh, Thomas, rotting flesh."

De'Ath slept uneasily that night. Any dream featuring Dredge was likely to veer to nightmare, given the extreme ugliness of his actual countenance. But a gang of ten Dredge mutants marauding your Shed was a vintage horror movie.

Bullock too was visting the kitchen for water throughout the night, although his restlessness was more the result of his bowl of durian, the 'King of Fruit'. Nevertheless, he was also aware of the prowlings of Dredge in his sleeping imagination.

Bullock telephoned De'Ath after breakfast. "Listen, Tom, are you going to the allotment today? Yes, I was too, this afternoon. Just a thought, but I thought we'd walk down together. Yes, strength in numbers… well, you never know, eh… come around mine about two."

A pasty-looking De'Ath arrived at 22 The Nook in a combat jacket and peaked cap. He looked like the aged Fidel Castro. By contrast, Bullock carried a silver-handled walking cane, an odd accessory to his regular gardening attire. The cane was part of his Sherlock Holmes fantasy and, like that of his hero, could be used to set about the sort of vagabond they might expect to encounter that day. They set off to the allotment with silent resolve. As they turned the corner and strode purposefully down the allotment track, they could see that their expected visitor had already arrived. A figure was reclining spread-eagled against the Shed, supping clumsily from a large plastic bottle. The pair looked at each other with concern, and marched forward. Dredge was surrounded by empty cider bottles and scattered chip papers. He was dribbling drool from an enormous wad of chewing tobacco pouched in his cheek. Bullock strode boldly towards the drunk. "Dredge, if you have damaged our estate, I will set about you, drunk or no, and despite your age!"

Dredge looked up with narrowing eyes and pointed at Bullock, gaping like a goldfish for several seconds before he spoke in a broken croak.

"You bastards. You blimmin' blabbed. Tilletson put me out. You bastard grasses! YOU GRASSING BASTARDS!" He hauled himself to his feet and and began to whirl around flailing his arms.

Bullock and Thomas were not quite sure what to do in the face of this unusual drunken rage. "Is he preparing for warfare, Tom? He recalls to me the Whirling Dervishes," Bullock suggested out of the corner of his mouth. De'Ath replied, also very quietly, and studying the whirling man intently.

"Well, I believe that the rotations of the Dervish dancers are more concerned with entering a religious trance in order to draw cosmic energies."

"Blimey. Mebbe he'll turn into the Hulk."

Dredge continued to spin, spewing loud oaths and dark brown drool. It was remarkable that he stayed upright. "It's like summat out of t'bloody Omen," remarked Bullock, leaning on his cane.

With all the fuss, Philp, who had been trimming the hawthorn hedge with a billhook, appeared from over the footbridge, still suffering badly from his allergy. "Dredge?" he called loudly. "What the hell are you doing making that racket here? Stop yer spinning, you prannet!"

Dredge slowed his circumlocutions like a braking merry-go-round. He peered in the direction of his interlocutor or rather, in his extreme drunken dizziness, his many interlocutors, who slowly, slowly, became one, then there was bleary recognition.

"Philp. You git. I forgot you gardened round here."

Philp strode nearer and stopped, ten yards from Dredge. Dredge seemed to sober up remarkably. "So it was you who grassed me, was it?" he spat. "Saw me making me delivery, eh?"

Philp took another eight, wordless strides towards the man he had known and quarrelled with since schooldays. "Might have been."

There was a long pause. Like two gunfighters, they stood, jaw to jaw. For Bullock, it was a scene straight out of 'The Good, the Bad and the Ugly'. He imagined the chiming of a pocket watch as they stood, eyes narrow, fingers twitching at their belts. As the music ended in Bullock's head, Dredge made his move. He sent his ancient hob-nailed boot smashing with bone-splintering force into Philp's spindly left shin. De'Ath and Bullock both winced at the crunching sound, which resounded over the entire allotment. Philp yowled like a tomcat and hopped around the ground in excruciating pain. Dredge cackled victoriously, hands on his knees.

Bullock decided to enter the fray, and marched up to Dredge, wielding his cane. "How dare you strike such a low blow to an old man! Get about your way, Dredge, before I call the police."

Dredge gobbed his tobacco defiantly at Bullock, but retreated towards his bicycle. "See you at the annual show, Philp," he croaked to the still-hopping Philp, whose swelling shin was being gingerly inspected by De'Ath. "I'll have more time to drub you this season, now I'm a man of leisure."

Philp pushed De'Ath away, hobbling after Dredge and apoplectic with rage. "What else did you sell to these pillocks, Dredge? DDT? Methyl bromide? Agent fucking Orange!!! I'll have the law on you, Dredge. But first I'll have you with me billhook!!" Picking up his razor sharp hedging tool, he limped crookedly up the path, as Dredge mounted his steed and pedalled for his life.

Bullock put his arm around De'Ath's shoulders, heading for the Shed. "Eh, you can see how wars start, eh, Thomas. Best leave 'em to it. Now then, where's that buzzard. That'll see t'pigeons off." He rummaged through a pile of boxes and other items and found the rubber sparrowhawk. He proceeded to nail it to the eaves of the Shed, where it perched, cockeyed.

Chapter Three

Summer

"It's not turning out to be much of a summer, love, is it?" Bella was boiling sprouts and carrots to a mush for dinner, or tea, as she called it. The kitchen air was thick with steam, cigarette smoke and a burning smell from a pair of lamb chops under an over-heated grill pan.

Basker, slumbering in his box as ever, raised a crumpled eyelid and flopped a paw on the lino. "If that woman carries on burning those chops, they'll be inedible, and they'll have to give them me," he thought, with relish.

"No, grey, cool, wet, not much difference to the other seasons really," replied Dot. "I'm just going to turn those chops down a bit, Bella. Ron's dinner will be burned to a cinder!"

Basker sighed. "Interfering busybody. Chum again, then." He went back to sleep, to dream of charred chops.

"Oh, yes, thanks love, they are getting a bit black. Anyway, you know how people are supposed to look like their dogs, well what if we were vegetables?" enquired Bella, lighting another Embassy. "My Ron would be a spud, wouldn't he? A great big King Edward!! What about your Tom?"

"Well, a leek , I suppose, or a runner bean."

"I'd be a turnip. Or a beetroot. What about you, Dot?"

"Well, I must admit, I'd prefer to be a flower, really, but if I had to choose, I hope I'd resemble a nice lettuce."

"Yes, I can see it. Lettuce you are. Well, I must say, I'm looking forward to me hols."

"Where are you off to then, Bella?"

"Marbella. For *three* weeks. I've never been on holiday for three weeks before. It seems excessive somehow, I almost feel a bit guilty."

"Now, that won't do, if anybody deserves three weeks in the sun it's you."

"Well, that's what Ron says. He says we've worked all our lives for this sort of leisure, and now we've got the time. Our Angeline is in time-share, she's got us this villa quite cheap. Are you going away, love?"

"Oh yes, Tommy and I usually go to this little place on the Dorset coast we like, and we go walking. Tommy doesn't like the sun… he comes out in this funny rash, and I don't like flying, so we generally have our Dorset break in September. But as you know, we like to have lots of long weekends, exploring Britain. So many places to see in our own country, it's enough for me and Tom."

"Oh, we just have to get our fix of the sun, Dot, and that means Spain. And we've mastered the language you see - well me, really, not Ron. I can order anything we want, in Spanish. I do think that's important, do you not?"

"Oh yes, it's very important. I hear stories of British people going to places, especially Spain, and just expecting the locals to speak in English. It is just insulting to them, isn't it?"

"Oh, you want to hear them!" said Bella, warming to her theme and draining the sprouts in a cloud of steam, "pig ignorant and proud, some of them. This bloke last year in Almeira kept shouting out to this handsome waiter 'Oi, garcon!' Well, I saw red, I went over to him and said, 'if you want to get the attention of our waiter, it's not garcon, it's 'camerero', and Spanish for please is 'per favor!' Well, would you believe it, the whole place clapped! This rough family walked out, and the manager came out a bit later and brought us a bottle on the house. Red wine, vino tinto. Here, hang on, I'll show you him, oh lovely man, Antonio, he was called, the waiter was his son." Bella was a racist in general, but loved the Spanish, believing Julio Iglesias to be the finest male of the species.

"Oooh, Bella, you are brave. I wouldn't dare do such a thing."

"You would, Dot, I'm sure you would. You'd stick up for what's right. See, there's Antonio and me. And that's the wine bottle he gave us, look, on the shelf. I kept it, as a reminder to speak out against rudeness."

"I do think it's the trouble with us English, we just don't speak up. Well, we will both miss you, but we are looking forward to entertaining Basker!"

"Oh it is good of you, that, Dot. You know he can go to Wendy's if he gets too much trouble. We put him in kennels one year, but it didn't suit him. Took a long time for you to forgive us for putting you in kennels that year didn't it, Baskerville?"

Baskerville woke again and looked up from his basket, alarmed. Kennels! He remembered kennels. "Bad place," he thought. "Treated like a dog there, I was." Baskerville didn't mind bumping into the odd dog now and again on his walks, and some he quite liked, but he thought of himself more as a person than a dog. He liked his home comforts. Sofas, the telly on, big gas fire. Nice walk to the newsagents. Kennels: constant barking, smell of disinfectant, route-marched in a chain gang by a severe kennel maid who told him he was spoiled and fat. He had told Bullock flat when he got back home, "No more kennels for me."

By odd coincidence, Baskerville's bad experience at kennels was the topic of conversation a quarter of a mile away in the Shed. "And I looked into those big sad eyes, Thomas, and they just said to me, 'don't even think of sending me there again!' So anyway, it is very good of you to have him. You should get yourself a hound, Watson."

"Well, I just might do that. We have been more cat people really, but after Kipper was run over last year, we were so upset that we haven't got another."

"Oh, hounds are much more fun than cats!" announced Bullock, with his usual assertiveness.

"And more work, I think. No, there's something pleasantly aloof about cats."

"Well, you see how you get on with old Basker. Bet says you'll be after a hound like him! Now, there's not a lot to do is there lad, on the patch. Bit of watering if if gets dry, bit of tidying up, that kind of thing."

"Yes, it's the time just to watch your garden grow. I hope it doesn't get too hot, and I shall just sit here and listen to the cricket." De'Ath seemed very satisfied with this prospect.

Bullock rustled about in his haversack. "Now, Tommy, I know you don't like these things, and neither do I much, but it's only like a walkie-talkie, eh?" he handed De'Ath a 'pay-as-you-go' mobile phone.

De'Ath sighed. "Well, I must say, I never really saw the point. Telephone boxes seem more than adequate."

"Aye, but, think on," insisted Bullock. "We can speak from Shed to poolside! I thought it would be good fun to talk. Just think of the modern marvel of communication. Shed in England to swimming pool in Spain! You could tell me the cricket score, and I could tell you the temperature! How about it, partner?"

"You're right, Ron, these little things have changed our world. In touch, anywhere, anytime. I just wish they would make less irritating noises."

"Well, you can choose, Tommy. I know the usual ones are crap, but you can download 'owt you want. Just press that button, then that one, that's it, now that one." The phone trilled a few bars of the theme tune for Gardeners World, much to the delight of Bullock. De'Ath, too, chuckled. "Well, must keep up with the times I suppose," said De'Ath, "and it will be good to keep you updated of events here. My goodness, this 'Menu' is complicated."

A couple of weeks later, after brewing a mug of tea, De'Ath settled down as the afternoon session began for the second day of the second Test match. The door of the Shed was open and a pleasant breeze blew through. He turned on the mobile phone and put it down on Bullock's seat. A few minutes later, and rather to De'Ath's surprise, the phone trilled its theme. "HELLO!" bellowed De'Ath.

"Eh up, lad, no need to shout, Tom. I can hear you fine. I'm floating about the pool in a big duck! With a pina colada!"

"Well, that certainly beats my mug of tea, Ron," chuckled De'Ath. "Is it as hot as I fear?"

"Bloody baking, mate. Bloody lovely. I've got me

Tilletson's hat on, t'keep sun off, though. What's it like back in Blighty?"

"I've got the pullover on. Not too hot, but quite humid. The atmosphere is quite heavy, you know. Ball swinging around at Lords." They discussed the Test match for a while and the promising growth of their leeks. "Oh yes, Philp has been popping by. Quite friendly actually. He was telling me a bit about the history of the Shed. An old friend of his, Fred Snow, used to garden your plot. He built the Shed, apparently. A pipe man. Died of lung cancer poor chap. Oh,no, Ron, I won't be giving up. You're at more risk in that hot sun. Be careful to use lots of Factor 25."

"Don't worry about me son, I look like I'm about to swim the channel. Basted with sun cream. Anyway, this is good fun, this, talking to you like you were on t' next sunbed. Have a good weekend, mate. You give me a call on Monday afternoon."

De'Ath chuckled as he switched off the telephone with a beep. Yes, it was amazing he thought, that you were able to have such clear conversations. How the air must be filled with waveforms. To think the first transatlantic telephone call only happened sixty-odd years ago. With the thought of waveforms from all over the planet buzzing about the allotment, he slowly nodded off to the sound of the long wave cricket commentary.

A while later, De'Ath's eyes opened. Sitting opposite him in Ron's armchair was an old man, smoking a briar pipe. He looked at De'Ath and nodded. He was wearing an old broad-knit yellow jumper that seemed to come down to somewhere near his knees, with holes in each elbow. De'Ath was surprised to have company, but not at all alarmed. No words seemed to be needed. The cricket commentary flowed mellifluosly on. The old man had very bushy white eyebrows. He nodded approvingly as an English batsman was announced to hit a four to the square leg boundary. He smiled kindly at De'Ath, moved his arm from side-to-side whilst waggling his fingers, and disappeared. Only now did De'Ath feel cold sweat and a slight panic. He closed his eyes and opened them again. Only the punctured armchair was there. He looked at his watch. He had been asleep half an hour or so. Perhaps he was still asleep and in one of those ultra-real dreams and would presently awake. He stood up and stepped out of the Shed. It was still humid and trying to rain. He sat down on the wooden threshold of the door, removed his glasses, held his head in his hands, and squeezed his eyes closed with his palms. He was fairly certain that he had just been sitting with a ghost. The ghost of Fred Snow, the builder and long-time occupier of the Shed.

De'Ath had never believed in ghosts. He had never enjoyed ghost stories and was completely sceptical of any claims of sightings. He began to shake and was suddenly in need of human company. He got up and walked over towards Philp's allotment. As he walked, legs wobbling slightly, he recalled that Philp had earlier that day told him of Fred, as he had reported to Bullock on the mobile phone. He considered the possibility that his sleeping mind had invented the vision or even, on waking, that there was some sort of subconscious invention. It might have been. But as he walked, he was still pretty certain that he had just been sitting with a ghost.

Philp was adjusting twine between his bean canes, as De'Ath approached. "Hello, Death, have you come to visit Philp the old Forker?"

"Mr. Philp, I am of the strong opinion that I have just been sitting in the Shed with the ghost of your old friend Fred."

Philp could tell from De'Ath's demeanour that this was not a prank or a joke. The two men looked at each other for a while and finally, Philp looked at the ground. "Come and sit down, lad, I think you've had a shock. And I want to see what a man who has just seen a ghost really looks like!"

De'Ath sat on the bench outside Philp's shed, whilst Philp fetched a flask and an old mug with Queen Elizabeth's Silver Jubilee on it. He poured the warm, strong tea into the mug for himself and the flask cup for De'Ath, which he took with slightly trembling hand. They sat in silence awhile, sipping tea and looking out on Philp's verdant allotment. "He just sat in Ron's chair. He was there when I came back from Nod. Not a dream, I'm pretty sure. Smoking a briar pipe, bushy eyebrows. Just sat, then smiled, then disappeared. Could have been ten seconds, but it was difficult to say." De'Ath took a shaky sip of tea.

"Smiled, did he?" asked Philp fondly.

"Yes, a warm smile, encouraging perhaps. He nodded at me also, as if to greet me. And I'm pretty sure he signalled four when Thorpe hit a boundary. He was wearing a long yellow pulley."

At this Philp started. "A yellow jumper? My God, that was Snowy alright!" He stood up. "You know De'Ath, when I was telling you about him earlier on?"

"Yes, I thought about that just now. I thought that might just have got rolled up in my sleep and imagination and, you know, projected somehow."

"I was thinking that too. Until you told me about his pullover. Snowy gardened in that jumper every day. He called it his gardening dress. It fell apart eventually. But, Tom, I'm certain I never told you about it this morning. And the cricket. Mad about cricket he was."

De'Ath gulped as Philp sat down again, excitedly. "Come on, I must go and look where you saw Snowy." He practically pulled De'Ath up, who rather reluctantly retraced his steps to the Shed. Philp sat down in De'Ath's chair. "He just materialised in that chair did he? Right, I'm going to see if Snowy will materialize for his old mate Don." Philp was a firm believer in ghosts, having claimed to see several, and often felt the presence of his dead wife about their home. He was sure that if Snowy was about, he would come to visit him.

De'Ath started to shake again and felt the need to explain these extraordinary events to Dot. "Well look, Mr. Philp, please feel free to stay there as long as you like. I'm off

home. Perhaps you could lock up when you're done."
"Yes, yes, I will. I'd better keep the cricket on. Maybe Snowy came to find out the score!"

De'Ath left, his head still full of wonder.

De'Ath was annoyed with Philp, on approaching the Shed the next morning, that he had not locked the door, which hung open. But on closer inspection, he noticed Philp's old boots on the floor and then the old man, fast asleep in the chair. He had kept vigil all night. De'Ath pottered about with the stove and kettle, the noises of which eventually roused Philp, who stretched blearily and farted loudly. "Bugger me, I've been here all night Death! And not a sign of bloody Snowy."

De'Ath was disappointed at this news. A sighting by Philp would have gone a long way to confirming his own. "Well, never mind, Mr. Philp. Dot was telling me that it can depend on exactly the right meterological conditions."

"I thought he'd come back and listen to the cricket with me. So, what do you think, are you still sure you saw him."

"I am still as certain as I can be, Mr. Philp. He seemed so interested in the cricket. He seemed to listen."

"Well, he was a cricket nut. Good player, they tell me, in his time. Always had the cricket on, did Snowy. Well, he never came to see me. I'd better get home and get a wash. I had a great sleep though. Perhaps he was watching over me, eh?"

"I am sure he was, Mr. Philp. Just wait till Ron hears about it. I'm not going to tell him on the phone though. Some things need to be explained in person."

A fortnight later, as July beagn to shine, a lobster-red creature in a sombero arrived back at the Shed. He beamed with pleasure at the way the allotment had grown. They were getting the hang of this gardening thing. From across the bridge, came Philp and De'Ath muttering conspiratorially.

"Tommy Boy, and Mr. Philp!!" shouted Bullock.

"Ron! Didn't expect you till tomorrow! Welcome home, old chap!" beamed De'Ath. Philp was less enamoured with Bullock's return, which he tried to make clear.

"Bloody hell, Bollock, just look at the colour of you man. You are making my beetroots look like spring onions. And what the Devil is that thing on your head?"

"Now then, lads, I've brought you both a nice sombrero to

keep the sun off. Here we are!" From a large yellow plastic bag, Bullock indeed produced two hats similar to his own, which he insisted they all wear.

"Caramba! Now we're three caballeros!!" he sang at the top of his voice, "Do you remember that one, Mr. Philp?"

"Donald Duck, wasn't it? Blimey that must have been one of Walt Disney's first Technicolor fillums."

"Yes, wasn't there a parrot as well? What was the other caballero?" pondered De'Ath.

"A rooster," replied Bullock. "The duck went onto superstardom, the parrot and the rooster just declined into drugs and drink."

"Well, thanks for the hat, Bollock, I'll leave you and your mate to catch up. There's been a bit of drama round here." Philp wandered back over the bridge in his enormous sombrero.

"Drama, Tommy, nothing untoward lad?"

"No, no, come and have a sit down, Ron, I'll tell you all about it."

De'Ath began to tell his ghostly Shed tale, with great seriousness. He was very disappointed, upon reaching the apparition part of the story, when Bullock fell into rather disparaging laughter. He was a firm non-believer in the supernatural. "Oh dear, Watson, your mind has been playing tricks whilst I were sunnin' meself. Sun got to you, lad! What absolute rubbish, ghosts! I thought you had a scientific mind, Tom."

De'Ath thought this rather rude, even for Bullock. "Well, that is how it happened. And you are right, until that moment, I didn't believe in ghosts. But I tell you, I saw what I saw."

"I reckon you've been spending too much time around that old spook Philp. Been filling your head with jollyrobbins, lad."

"Well, tell me what I saw then, Sherlock."

"I will, I will, Watson. Several Sherlock stories on the unravelling of the 'supernatural'. Now, as I recall, you were telling me Philp was hanging about, telling you all about this bloke. You fell asleep and had a dream about him. Simple."

"No, not so simple, Ron," replied De'Ath patiently, filling a bowl of tobacco, "I saw details that I couldn't possibly know. A long yellow gardening pullover. His interest in cricket."

"You're sure that Philp didn't tell you beforehand?"

"No."

"Well. Maybe you've seen a picture of him at the Reading Room?"

De'Ath considered this with interest. "Hmmm, that is a possibility. I will ask Mr. Philp to come over with me and have a look at those old pictures. I'll do that this afternoon."

Philp and De'Ath were on their way back to the allotment after a visit to the village hall. There had indeed been a picture of Fred Snow at an annual gardening show, but he had been in collar and tie, not in his yellow gardening 'dress'. The visit had reinforced in De'Ath's mind that the face he saw was Snowy. The pair was in deep discussion about the details of the garment as they walked. As they approached the Shed, all was quiet, and the Shed was locked. Suddenly, a ghastly figure in a mustard jersey leapt into their path from the hedgerow with a shriek. "BOOOO!!!" went the figure.

"AAAARGGGH!!!" went Philp, sinking to his knees in fear and holding his head in his hands. De'Ath simply froze in his tracks. It only took a few moments to realize that the figure was Bullock with flour all over his face, wearing a rather tight mustard jumper, borrowed from Bella. He shook with laughter.

"You silly fucker, Bullock, you could have scared us both to death... and I'll tell you what... I *will* fucking haunt you!!" shouted Philp, getting to his feet.

"Yes, that wasn't well appreciated, Ron," added De'Ath, still hearing his heart thudding in his ears.

However, the prank was still being warmly appreciated by Bullock himself. But not for long. Out of the corner of his eye, Philp saw a watering can half-full of water. With Bullock still heaving with laughter, Philp was able to dart over, pick up the can, and throw the water in Bullock's face, just as he rose from holding his knees, with another gale of laughter. "There, that'll wash the smile off your face," said Philp with satisfaction. Bullock grimaced. With white flour pasted to his face, and water dripping from his ears, he resembled a dishevelled Oliver Hardy.

"Right. Water fight," he announced quietly.

As the trio chased each other around the allotment with buckets of water and hoses for the next hour, gasping with laughter, there was little question that they had regressed to the age of boys around a paddling pool. As they sat in the sun, all drenched and happy, the ghost of Fred Snow, puffing his briar pipe, watched beaming from the Shed.

It was proving a predictably difficult summer for Tilletson's. The balance sheet was getting worse, two people had been retired and one fired. Percy Tilletson was at his cluttered and soily desk, reading an aggresive letter from Marcus McMeddler. It was his last chance, the letter was telling him, in exotic grammar, to sell up. Tilletson screwed up the letter, and threw it in the bin. The dawn broke. He had been at his desk all night, working over and over at his account ledgers. He could see no way forward. Tilletson picked up his W.W. Greener 16-Bore Box-lock Ejector shotgun left to him by his father, which he had removed from its canvas bag. He ran his finger over the trademark elephants of the lock silver. From his desk drawer, he removed a box of shotgun cartridges. He looked dishevelled and disturbed as he ushered his dogs into the Volvo and laid his gun on the back seat. As he left the nursery at speed, it was uncharacteristic of him not to have stopped to lock the nursery gates.

"You see, it's all about manners for me, Dot. People think that Ron is rude, but he's not. He's forthright, but he is very well mannered actually. And all my children, I've brought them up the same. The English used to rule the world in manners, but it pains me to say it, the foreigners have much nicer manners. Well, not the Germans or French, obviously, but the Spanish, for example. Oh, lovely folk. Do you know, I could live out there. We talked about it, Ron and me."

"Yes, I agree, Bella. There are some rough, offensive folk about. Well, that's partly the reason that Tommy and I keep ourselves to ourselves. Quite happy in our own little world." Dot stroked the ears of Basker, who sat at her feet.

"I just don't think things are changing for the better. I mean, they all have two cars, the wives all work, but are they happy? No. They just want more," said Bella, getting into her stride. They were having a cup of tea in Bella's kitchen;

Tom and Ron were in the lounge studying road maps. "I am looking forward to our day out together. What is this place called again?"

"The 'Vegetable Experience', apparently."

"What, a bit like the Eden Project is it?"

"Well, not so tasteful, I wouldn't have thought, Bella. I believe it's more of a theme park. American owned apparently."

Bullock barged into the kitchen dressed smartly in a checked shirt and tie, kicking Basker accidently, who looked up at him contemptuously. "I do wish he would not wear shoes in the house," he thought.

"Sorry old Basker. Bit clumsy… well, it's a bit early for me these days tha' knows, eight o' clock, Dot!"

"What is this place all about again, Ron?" inquired Bella, lighting up an Embassy.

"Oh, well, apparently it is like Disneyland, only all about vegetables. Instead of Mickey Mouse, there's Kate the Carrot, Lesley Leek, that kind of thing, a museum of vegetables, an exhibition of vegetables, a giant cinema screen…"

"Is there a café?" interjected Bella.

"A café, love, oh yes, there's a café, restaurant – well veggie restaurant, like…"

"Good, that's all I need. Long as there's a café. Let's be off to Veggieland then!"

De'Ath was still looking worriedly at a road atlas.

"Come on, old lad, we've been through the route a dozen times. You navigate, I will drive." Bullock opened the back passenger door of his Rover, cleaned and waxed the previous evening, ushered Dot gallantly to her seat and ran round to do the same for his wife at the other side.

"Such a gentleman, your Ron, Bella!" commented Dot.

"Oh, aye, well house trained, he is… Ron, can we not bring Basker?"

"Oh no love, there's nowt for dogs there. We'll bring 'im summat back from t'shop. Bound to be a souvenir shop. Come on, Tom, will you put that map down? I know the way practically! Come on son, you put your feet up in the owd Rover."

The day-trippers were soon on their way. Basker ambled into the living room and lolloped onto his favourite chair. "Could have left the telly on for me," he thought. "He's right though, not for dogs these places. Still, I wouldn't mind a new squeaky toy from the shop. Hope they remember." And then he went to sleep.

"I told you, Ron. You should have gone left a mile back!" De'Ath was quietly losing his temper. They had been travelling for well over two hours and, by his calculations, should have been at the 'Vegetable Experience' already.

"Alright, alright, I'm turning round," muttered a perspiring Bullock.

"I'm sure we've been on this road before," said Bella, unhelpfully. "I'm dying for a smoke, get us there quickly, Ron."

"I'm sure I saw one of those brown signs back there," offered Dot.

"That was for the 'World of Cobbling' my love," corrected De'Ath.

"Load of cobblers, did you say, Tommo? Yes that about describes your navigational skills!"

"How hang on a minute, Ron..."

"Stop arguing boys, you're spoiling our day out, aren't they Dot... hang on, I can see a great big carrot..."

"Gosh, you're right," said Dot peering out of the window. "I thought it was a church spire. It is a sixty-foot carrot. Not very orange though. More like one of those mucky ones you get at the organic shop." The centrepiece of Vegetable Experience had seen better days. The wind, rain and lack of maintenance had taken their toll, and the paint had worn away in peeling patches down to grimy plastic.

"We've been bloody past it twice!" exclaimed Bullock, pulling into an unsignposted lane that led to an unpaved car park with a few scattered parked vehicles. A man in a radish costume sat slumped in a plastic garden chair smoking a cigarette. Seeing new visitors, he quickly stubbed it out and hurried towards the car. "Eh, up, it's Sir Reginald Radish!" said Bullock, grinning broadly.

"Well hello, hello, folks, just wonderful to see you all today. Park your car, er, anywhere you like, and come on in and veg out!" offered the radish.

"Thanks, Sir Reg," said Bullock, still delighted, as he parked the car. "Have you seen him on the advert, girls?"

"What advert?" asked Bella, climbing out of the car and immediately lighting up.

"Have you not seen the advert for this place on telly? Oh, it's brilliant. They only show it at odd times, like. Cartoon vegetables. Sir Reginald Radish is ruthless! Water, fertiliser, sunlight - he wants it all - and what Reggie wants, Reggie takes. Grow like weeds you know, radishes do!"

"Well, ours didn't do any good, Ron," objected De'Ath, closing the car door.

"Aye, well can't say I'm so bothered. They repeat on me. I likes a radish, but the radish don't like me, unfortunately."

"Oh, and me, Dot," joined Bella, "oh dear, they do make me burp, radishes."

"Oh, I love a radish myself. Lots of salt, delicious. A Swedish aquaintance of mine has them for breakfast," replied Dot.

"Breakfast?!" said Bullock, perplexed. "Are you sure, Dot, a radish...for breakfast?"

"Quite sure."

"Well I never. Radishes for breakfast. I'm going to ask Reggie. These blokes are all trained gardeners y'know. You can ask 'em anything you want. Did you hear that, Sir Reggie?" The party was striding towards the entrance of The Vegetable Experience. The sign was missing every 'e'.

On closer inspection, Sir Reginald Radish looked rather careworn. He looked like a clapped out provincial actor, which was precisely what he was. "What was that about me, my friends? You know, what Reggie wants, Reggie takes!" the actor ventured with a trained resonant voice, accompanied by a camp stage wink.

"They eat you for breakfast in Sweden, tha' knows! Did you know that Reggie?" Bullock was already posing for a photograph, with his arm round the radish, Bella squinting purposefully through her point-and-shoot.

The actor considered this; he was supposed to know about radishes, but had just finished his week as Lesley Leek, and had forgotten his radish facts. "Erm, yes, I, believe that is the case, well why not, a radish is good at, er, anytime?"

"Why not?" exclaimed Bullock, "I'll tell thee why not, lad. You've just had a nice bowl of Frosties and a cup of tea, perhaps you're thinking about some toast or a bacon buttie, and some blonde bird comes up and offers you a radish. Well, that's the last thing you'd want. That's why not. Have you been to Sweden?"

The actor had been to Sweden, on a Strindberg study week. "I have."

"And did you have radishes for breakfast?"

"No."

"Were you offered radishes for breakfast?"

"Well…"

"You weren't, were you?"

"No, but I had a boiled egg with fish paste in it," blurted the actor in desperation.

Bella had had enough of this stupid conversation and said so. "Come on Ronnie, we are all off to the caffy for a coffee."

"You don't look much like a gardener to me," growled Bullock to the radish. "Show us your hands."

Sir Reggie had on large green feathery gloves. "Not allowed to take me leaves off, sir."

"Oh, aye, very conveni…" Bullock was now being dragged by the neck to the visitor centre entrance by his wife.

"Thirty two pounds?" De'Ath was exclaiming at the kiosk.

"Are you OAPs?" enquired the woman in the kiosk, dressed as an onion.

"*We* are!" shouted Bella, pointing at Dot. "The fellers are still underage."

"Right, well twenty-eight pounds then please."

"Bloody 'ell, Ollie Onion," snorted Bullock, "I 'ope it's all in for that!"

Collecting their tickets, they went through a ticket barrier and into a desolate looking concrete arena, at the middle of which was the giant carrot. Many stalls lined the outside of the arena, but most appeared to be closed. They were approached by a burly potato. "Fancy a go on me stall, folks?"

"What do you have to do?" enquired Bella.

The potato handed her five plastic new potatoes. "Knock the flowerpots over and win a fluffy vegetable."

"Oh, go on Ronny, win us a fluffy cabbage. Eeh, it's just like Blackpool, this," Bella cackled excitedly.

Bullock took the objects in his podgy paw and drew back one in his right arm to throw. But the potato caught his wrist.

"Sorry guv, three quid."

"Three quid?!" exclaimed Bullock, "we've just paid thirty quid to get in!! I thought it was all in?"

"Everything but the stalls, sir."

Bullock wearily drew some change from his pocket.

"Here. Now how many of those pots do I have to knock over to win a cabbage?"

"Three mate."

Bullock hurled the potato and hit a pot fair and square in

the middle, but it failed to budge.

"Swizz!" shouted Bella.

"Is that bloody pot glued on?" demanded Bullock.

The human potato looked on glumly. "Got to throw it harder than that mate."

Bullock threw the remaining objects with great fury, but little accuracy, and they thudded against the back canvas. The potato cheered up at Bullock's failure. "Bad luck, sir. Try again?"

"Try again asking me and I'll have you up before the Trading Standards," responded Bullock in sullen fury. "How about a consolation prize? My dog would enjoy one of those squeaky toys there."

"Oh go on then. Squeaky parsnip man for you." The potato handed over a plastic object balefully to Bella.

"Good, that's Basker taken care of," said she, putting the object in her huge handbag, "it's time for coffee." The four made their way to the tea shop. The interior resembled a self-service motorway restaurant, except that plastic vegetable mobiles hung from the ceiling, and the tables were of the rustic picnic style. Few were occupied.

"Sit down, ladies, choose us a nice table and me and Tom'll sort the elevenses out."

A young woman in a lurid green polo shirt was standing at the till inspecting her false nails.

"Aye, we'll have two coffees and two teas, please love, and

four slices of this carrot cake," requested Bullock politely.

"If you'd like to help yourself, sir," replied the woman unhelpfully, turning her head to look at nothing in particular in the other direction.

"Oh, right, yes...get us a tray then, Tommo." Bullock squinted at a machine with a number of numerical options. "Right, er, cappuccino, 54, right, 5, 4..." A frothy liquid gurgled out of a spigot and into the draining grid.

"Put the cup in first, sir" offered the woman impatiently.

"Right, yes. Let's try again, with a cup. How, how does one get a cup of tea, I don't see that option here?" asked Bullock, red-faced.

"Tea bags in front of you, hot water option 43," advised the woman mechanically.

After several dithering efforts, Bullock and De'Ath endeavoured to fill their tray with two mugs of boiling cappuccino, two large styrofoam beakers of tepid water each with a tea bag on a string, many small cartons of milk and sugar sachets, and four plates of aged carrot cake wrapped in clingfilm. The till woman tapped her computerised till joylessly. "Thirteen pounds forty please."

"What??" exploded Bullock, "Thirteen quid? Sorry love, you must have made a mistake. How much have I paid for this cup of water and a tea bag?"

"One seventy-five," replied the woman without expression, handing over the till receipt. Bullock strongly considered leaving the sad contents of the tray where they were and storming off, but Bella was shouting at him.

"Come on love, I'm parched out!!"

Bullock grudgingly handed over notes to the now smiling cashier. "Don't drop that tray, Tom, I'll have to get an overdraft if you do," muttered Bullock, carefully checking his change.

"Eeeh, that's a nice cappucinno," said Bella, beaming as she attacked the froth with a tea spoon. Bullock glumly dunked his tea bag up and down into the beaker.

"Now, I can buy a tea bag for about 2p and boil a kettle of water for about 4p. Milk, sugar, carton, penny each. So I reckon the mark up on this cuppa is £1.65. Not bad business that. Bloody criminal, actually. Bloody usury. "

"Stop moaning about money, Ron, you are ruining our day!" admonished Bella, carrot cake all over her top lip. "Drink yer tea up, the show is on in five minutes."

"The all-singing, all-dancing Vegetable Experience show will take place in the Central Arena in five minutes," added the tannoy, on cue.

"Oh, this sounds good, eh Tom?" said Bullock, managing half his tea in one grimacing gulp.

"Mmm, I wonder if I can bring my coffee with me?" said De'Ath, beginning a sip of his scalding drink.

"Oh aye, bring it, come on," said Bullock rising.

But the cashier was on them, even as they rose.

"No crockery in the Central Arena," she admonished, sternly.

"Oh, I'll just finish it here, then," offered De'Ath deferentially.

"Well you don't want to miss the show. There's only two a day you know." The young woman continued her lecture as she began to clear the cups, which had been drained.

"Oh, well, I'll leave it then, eh?" said De'Ath, laughing nervously.

"No you bloody won't, Tom…we'll sit here and wait till you've finished your coffee. Leave those cups where they are, young lady."

There then passed three minutes of odd silence. Bullock looked sternly at the tea woman, who seemed to be waiting for them to leave. The tea woman looked at De'Ath, drumming her long nails on the back of his chair. Dot put her hand protectively on De'Ath's thigh. Bella lit up. De'Ath took quick sips off his boiling coffee and laughed nervously again after each sip. He wondered how on earth Bella had quaffed this searing liquid. At length, De'Ath decided to go for it and down the last quarter of his cup. It was a mistake. The coffee was still just too hot and jumping to his feet, he simultaneously gave the table such a jolt as to send cups and saucers flying, and he coughed his coffee in a fine mist over the entire party. He collapsed back into his chair, spluttering and coughing. Dot set about patting him on the back and Bella began to clean everybody up with a wad of tissues collected from the basement of her huge handbag.

Bullock sprang up red in the face. "That was your bloody

fault!" he shouted at the tea woman, who had escaped most of the coffee spray.

"Don't you shout at me! Look at the mess he's made. Look, these cups are all broken!" she returned, hands on hips.

Bella took control. "And you can tidy them up. If you had any manners you'd apologise for being a madam." She swept her party imperiously away, leaving the woman to mutter about OAPs under her breath.

"Oh dear," De'Ath was still spluttering as he walked, "I am sorry, I caused quite a scene. I am very sorry, everyone."

"Weren't your fault, Tommy!" said Bullock, with the ladies nodding in agreement.

"Is your mouth burned, Tommy?" fussed Dot.

"Well, it is tingling a bit, I must admit," replied De'Ath fingering his roasted upper palate.

"Here, love," said Bella, rummaging in her voluminous handbag, "have a Fox's Glacier Mint. That will sooth yer mouth."

"Oh, yes, thanks Bella, that's just the ticket."

At the entrance to the arena, a woman dressed as a watermelon requested their pass tickets, which Bella produced. "Anywhere you like, my loves, show is about to start. Would you like programmes?" enquired the melon.

"Oh, I think so!" said Bella enthusiastically.

"Three pounds please."

"Three..." spluttered Bullock.

"Ron!" warned Bella, "two please, love."

"One thanks," said Bullock quietly, handing the melon woman the right money.

The four took their seats on the circular benches surrounding the central arena. A scattered audience of about fifty folk looked on expectantly, as a crescendo of piped music erupted. De'Ath, as he sucked his mint loudly, was studying the progamme, a pamphlet of stapled bright yellow photocopied pages. "The music is especially composed by a Czech modernist, and is entitled 'Bounty of the Garden'." he informed his party.

"Sounds like they are tuning up," commented Dot.

The discordant music increased to an uncomfortable volume. Bella covered her ears.

"Christ, what a din!" shouted Bullock, "this is why I never listen to bloody Radio 3!"

"I think it is rather interesting," offered De'Ath, thoughtfully.

"Oooh, look up there," yelled Bella, "are they peas or sprouts?"

"Sprouts, I think," said Dot.

She was correct; a tribe of Brussel sprout men began to abseil from hatches opening at the top of the carrot pillar.

Simultaneously, marrow people began to roll from the edge of the arena, and beetroots began to emerge from traps in the stage. Before long, the pillar and arena was alive with all manner of vegetable people, writhing, leaping and pratfalling with abandon.

"Good Lord, this is most disconcerting," declared Bullock.

But De'Ath was on his feet, grinning and applauding. He laughed loudly as a gang of tomatoes threw themselves at the carrot pillar and bounced off comically. Then, at the height of the frantic activity, an enormously loud cymbal crashed, making the sparse audience wince, and the vegetable players collapse. A sombre drum began, and a host of black-clad creepy-crawlies - caterpillar, fly and bug people - entered the arena and began attacking the crops. "Ho, ho," winked Bullock, "we know all about this lot, eh, Tom?" De'Ath was nodding and grinning stupidly.

The insects attacked the plants for what seemed an age of monotonous drumming. Most of the audience began to check their watches. Finally, a number of white-clad performers entered the arena with large bug guns and began to despatch the pests, which either died instantly or ran off. Incongruously, the piped music changed to upbeat Elgar. A huge banner was unfurled by the bug slayers, as the vegetables perked up and began embracing or dancing with their saviours. The banner, in huge red letters, announced 'INFESTOS KILLS ALL KNOWN BUGS. DEAD.' As the players took their bows and a ripple of polite applause, an announcement was made over the PA. "We would like to thank Infestos, the sponsors of this drama. Infestos kills all known bugs. Dead." Bullock and De'Ath looked at each other incredulously.

"Is that what you use then Tommy, Infestos?" asked Dot, still politely clapping.

"No it is not, my love!" replied De'Ath.

"Hardly encourages organic gardening, does it?" said Bella, lighting up.

Bullock began to shake his head. "Well, that's right love, but it wouldn't be so bad if it actually worked! It's rubbish, is Infestos."

As they trooped out of the arena, one of the white clad players ran athletically towards them with a basket of plastic bottles. "Please take a bottle of Infestos with our compliments," he gushed theatrically.

Bullock looked at the man in his Lycra bodysuit. "Gardener are you, son?"

"Oh yes, a horny-handed son of toil," responded the dancer/actor with a grin.

"How old are you son?"

"22?"

"Got a garden have you?"

"Well, more of a window box really, I live in Finchley, you see, and…"

"A window box? Don't tell me you spray that with Infestos?"

"Well, I do, occasionally, when I get an outbreak of, what was it now, er, early blighter?" the dancer tried hopefully.

"Well, I'll tell you what, lad when your pansies start giving you trouble, pour cold tea on 'em…be more use than that stuff!!" Bullock and De'Ath guffawed together, rather pompously. The dancer looked rather crestfallen.

"Give me that then, love," Bella said, taking the sample, feeling sorry for the young dancer, who smiled gratefully and bounded off. "Eeeh, yer a know-all Ronny, I'll give it to Wendy, she has all sorts of flies in her garden."

"Not surprised all that rubbish they cook, anyhow, it's dangerous for kids spraying that stuff about…" but, Bullock continued in a low whisper to De'Ath, "…mind you, like Lucozade next to the stuff we had a go with!" and the two fell to more conspiratorial guffawing.

"Come on," said Bella taking Dot's arm, "let's have a look in the shop."

"Oh, love, would you mind if Tom and I went into the Vegetable Museum instead. You know we hate shopping."

"Yes, alright then love, we don't mind do we Dot? We'll meet you here in half an hour."

The Vegetable Museum was a huge hangar, which one entered via an external metal spiral staircase. At the top of the stairs, Bullock and De'Ath paused to get their breath, then entered the metal door.

"Wow!!" said De'Ath with a grin.

"Crikey!!" added Bullock.

They were on the top shelf of a 'garden shed', which had been scaled to give the impression that they were the size of mice. Huge models of spades and forks hung from the walls, clay flower pots six feet high were stacked below. A huge moneyspider on a steel cable "thread" was being hauled up and down by an electric winch. "This is most impressive!" marvelled Bullock. "Things are looking up!"

Visitors were encouraged to walk the 'shelves' and examine the many museum exhibits on the walls and cases, then to descend to the next level of shelves by wooden steps. The men found the exhibits to be very absorbing. They examined the 'origin of vegetable section', noting their wild relatives. "Just to think, Tom, that we get great caulies and cabbages from what used to be these spindly-looking things," he remarked, looking at some tiny crucifers in a glass herbarium.

"Oh yes, we have a lot to thank Mendel for."

Bullock looked at De'Ath quizzically. "Do you mean Mendeleev? We're not going to go through that Mengele business again, are we?"

"No, no Ron," said De'Ath, bending to hold his knees with a grin, "Gregor Mendel, father of plant breeding. Come, here he is." De'Ath led Bullock to a portrait of an Augustinian monk.

"See here, he did experiments on peas, to prove that it was genetic inheritance and not the circumstances that a plant grew up in that determined how the next generation was."

Bullock studied the various charts and photographs. "Well that's not right that, Tom. It stands to reason, if you water and feed one plant, and ignore another, then the first one will produce the best seeds."

"No, it doesn't work like that. The genes that a plant inherits don't change. It doesn't matter what happens during a life. Genes stay same."

"Can't be right. If… if you water and feed one plant, and ignore another, then the first one will produce the best seeds."

"Yes, but that is only because you have allowed it to express its genes by giving it a good life. You starved the other one and prevented it from getting to maturity!"

"Proves me point."

"No, this won't do. I know you to be a man of science and deduction, and I can prove to you the theories of Darwin and Mendel over Lamarck…" The argument was becoming quite heated, and it was interrupted by an American in a roll-neck sweater.

"How are you boys enjoying the Museum?" he asked. "Sounds like you sure know your botany!"

"Well, one of us does," replied De'Ath rather tersely, who was not pleased at what he regarded as a rude interruption from a stranger.

Bullock was equally irritated by the interruption of an

argument he was positive about winning, but curious about the rude American. "You're not after three quid, are you?"

"John P. Reno, of Twapshank Associates. We have sponsored one of the exhibits downstairs," he said, extending his hand.

"A brilliant concept, the scale shed, we like it, Mr P. Reno. Ronald T. Bullock. And this is Mr. Thomas S. De'Ath."

"Nice to make your aquaintance, boys," he replied, shaking hands first with the vice and then with the bream. "Well, in the States it would have to be a garage, you know. But you Brits, you like your little huts, huh?"

"Aye, we prefer a shed to a ranch, if that's what you mean?"

"Hey, don't get me wrong boys! Ain't nothin' wrong sittin' out on the verandah in a rockin' chair jes' watchin' that old squash patch grow!"

"Playing a banjo perhaps?" sneered De'Ath.

Reno hee-hawed like a donkey. "You sure got my number there, mister, now you KNOW I'm from the south, how DID you know that?" The American's easy affability was beginning to thaw the Englishmen's distaste, and they both laughed a little.

"Now come on boys, now you will excuse me eavesdroppin' on your little discussion about Mr. Mendel here." He pointed to the portrait of the monk, continuing, "fact is, we have well and truly consigned Mr. Mendel to history. Old genetic breeding, out! New genetic engineering, in! Let me show you the REAL exhibit in this show!"

The dapper American led the pair down two flights of wooden stairs to the floor of the 'shed', where a row of fairground cars in the kidney shape of beans stood within a cavern marked, 'The Future of Gardening, sponsored by Twapshank Associates.' "Climb aboard, boys," said Reno, opening the door of one of the carts. "This way the future lies!"

Climbing in beside them, he pressed a button on a remote control device, and the cart rattled and rumbled into a dark tunnel ahead. Bullock recognised the narrator of the show as the deep ham actor voice of all US movie trailers. "Imagine a garden where the plants grow taller on less water. Where the crop is greater on less fertilizer. Where plants grow pest-free without chemical spray. Twapshank Associates bring you that reality. You tell us the seeds you want…and we make 'em!"

The carts then rumbled forward again. A large TV screen lit up to one side of them, and a goofy looking Jewish American began waving to them. "Hee-eey!"

"Hey, Ross!" laughed Reno. "Say hi to Ross, fellers!"

"Er, good afternoon Ross," offered Bullock.

The figure on the TV screen turned towards Bullock and waved. "Hee-eey!"

Reno laughed again. "Clever, huh. And you don't know

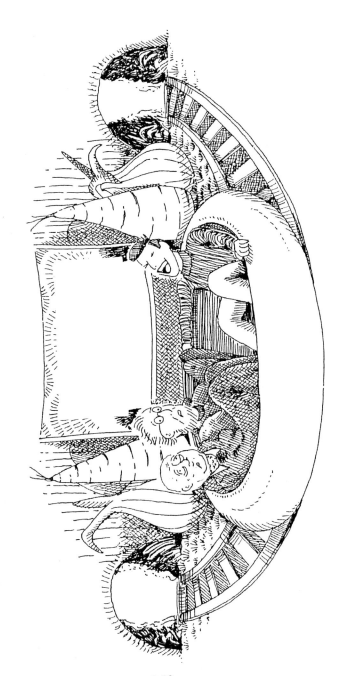

who it's going to be! It could be Monica or Joey. Or Chandler. Any of 'em!"

"Any of who?" said De'Ath, looking at Bullock, who shrugged his shoulders.

"Well, the cast of 'Friends', that's who!" exclaimed Reno, looking perplexed.

"Oh, that's a kid's programme on telly isn't it?" said Bullock. "Or one of those meant for both children and retarded adults?"

Reno looked concerned. "I'm getting the impression that our market researchers have got it all wrong over here. I thought everyone knew Ross!"

"You'd have been better using characters from Camberwick Green...or Trumpton!" offered De'Ath.

"Excuse me?" said Reno, "A soap, huh?"

"Well, not exactly a soap," explained De'Ath frowning, "but the characters pop up from a musical box. You never knew if it would be Dr. Mopp, or Mrs Honeyman, or whoever. It was usually Windy Miller."

Reno leaned back in the cart, looking deflated. It was not proving easy to convince British gardeners of the merits of genetically modified seeds. Nevertheless, he stabbed another button on his remote. Ross began to talk to them again. "Hey you wanna plant which grows tall and stong and gives you beans all summer long? Hey, no problem!

Twapshank bring you Superbeans. Whoah!" There was prolonged theatre laughter as a fast growing bean coiled round Ross' neck and pulled him over. He got up again, and wagged his index finger at the gyrating plant. "Wow, you are one amazing beanstalk!"

A blonde woman with high cheekbones entered the play to great applause. "Oh, oh, like, what *is* that plant, Ross?

"Oh hi, Phoebs. I'd like you to meet my Twapshank Superbean. Do you know this bean has been genetically altered to produce up to 100% more beans than a regular plant?" Loud theatre applause burst out.

"Oh oh, OK, that's like, sooo unnatural?"

"C'mon Phoebs! Doncha wanna feed the world's poor with improved plant breeding technology?"

"Oh, yeah, that would be cool. I guess?"

"You'd guess right, sweedie," replied Ross. Putting their arms around each other, the actors looked candidly and doe-eyed at the camera and recited in unison, "If you want to save the world, then buy Twapshank product today." The screen went blank, but a moment later a screen lit up on the other side and a craggy face winked at them. "Now, boys, tell me you know who this is?" said Reno, hopefully.

"Oh aye, I know who that is," grinned Bullock, "good afternoon Mr. Heston."

Charlton Heston inclined his face to Bullock and began to

speak. The camera panned back to reveal the veteran actor was walking in some kind of prairie dustbowl. "Y'know friends, my grandfather farmed these lands with seeds which often did not germinate. Plants that died at the first sign of drought. Poor harvests drove my forebears off this land in times of depression. What my old granddaddy would have given for a handful of Twapshank wheat or corn seeds. Reliable. Strong. Prolific. Do yourself a big favour. Buy Twapshank product today."

"More your kinda guy, Mr. Bullock?" enquired Reno, as the cart rolled on.

"Oh aye, I like Charlton! What other advocates can pop up on that screen then?"

"We have endorsements from Ronnie Reagan, we have Whoopie Goldberg and we have Michael Jackson," said Reno proudly. "Do you know that Michael has created a completely genetically modified garden at his own home, exclusively using Twapshank Superseeds?"

"Well, I'll tell thee what, lad, if Mr. Jackson would like to come to our Shed and spend five minutes explaining this 'genetically improved' stuff, well, we'd make him welcome, tha' knows. Wouldn't we Thomas?"

"Oh yes, we'd make him a mug of tea alright. He'd have to put up with our pipe tobacco of course. However, I understand he wears a surgical mask, so he would be OK for a bit," said De'Ath thoughtfully.

"Yes, well, let's move along to the rest of the exhibition," said Reno wearily, but Bullock was looking at his watch.

"Oh, I'm sorry Mr. Reno, we must meet our good lady wives very shortly. You'll have to speed us through I'm afraid. But we could return this afternoon, my wife would enjoy meeting Whoopie Goldberg, I feel certain."

"Oh, sure, sure," replied Reno. They sped rapidly past many other chambers extolling the merits of GM. "Well, it sure was nice to meet you," said Reno genuinely, ushering the pair from the cart. "And please, before you leave, a small token from Twapshank Associates." He handed over two packets of seeds.

"I hope you gennelmen will plant those seeds and give them a try," he said with a bow. They shook hands, and the pair hurried out, conscious they were rather late.
Bella stood with bags bulging with crude paraphernalia from the shop. Dot was wearing a surprisingly tasteful silver necklace of tiny bean leaves, flowers and pods. "What have you got in those packets, Mr. Bullock?"

"I shall explain, Mrs. Bullock, over lunch, and you shall see for yourself later. A very interesting experience."

"But first, our vegetarian lunch," said De'Ath. "My turn to pay, please. To The Vegeraunt!"

"Well, that were much better than I thought it was gonna be," said Bullock, finishing his ice cream with fresh vanilla pods and dabbing his mouth with a paper serviette. "I always think veg is best served up with some meat or fish, but fair play, that meatloaf was pretty edible."

"Oh, me and Tom go vegetarian at least twice a week, don't we Tommy?" replied Dot.

"Eeeeh, poor olt Tommy," laughed Bullock, poking De'Ath in the ribs, "no wonder he's got no meat on him. Wouldn't do a thing like that to Mr. Bullock, eh Bella?"

"No chance," said Bella, "I did enoy that spinach omelette and chips, though. And your vegetable pastie was delicious, Dot."

"Yes, do you know, I'm going to buy their cookbook and try that one."

Debate had raged over the soup about the merits of genetic modification. They had all agreed that it wasn't right to have cows make plastic in their milk, but they were divided on GM crops. Dot was set against, De'Ath was on the fence, whilst the Bullocks were enthusiastic. "Anyway, let's have a look at these 'super-seeds' they gave you, then," said Bella. Bullock took the two packets he'd been given by Reno and put them on the table.

"Twapshank Superseeds All Expectations," Dot was reading. "Runner beans, variety, Invincible. Genetically modified to resist all known herbicides." What is the point of that then?"

"Ah, you see, my love, you plant them, then spray the ground with herbicide. They grow, everything else dies. No weeds."

"Oh, dear," said Dot looking worried, "they sound like Triffids!"

"Oh, that scared me to death, that film," said Bella.

"I don't think I ever saw it," said Bullock, inspecting the seed packet closely, "I vaguely remember the book though. Large broccoli-like plants, mutations from a meteor shower, start to attack and kill people, wasn't it?"

"Howard Keel. Kills 'em with seawater in the end." said Bella.

"That's right, Bella," said De'Ath who was stroking his beard thoughtfully. "What I remember about that movie was the geography of London was all wrong."

"Really, how do you mean?" asked Bella.

"Well, when Howard Keel leaves the Eye Hospital in Shoreditch… do you remember, Bella, he was the only one who wasn't blinded by the meteor, because his eyes were bandaged after an operation?" Bella nodded.

"Yes, he leaves Moorfields, then he turns a corner and he's in Lincoln's Inn Fields where he sees a dog being killed by a Triffid. Then he exits the park and he's in Victoria Station. Impossible! All these locations are several miles apart." De'Ath leaned back in his chair impassively. Bella was unusually lost for words. Dot looked on with silent pride.

Bullock hadn't really been listening; he was peering at the seeds in the packet he had opened with some caution. "Aye, well, in the book, sea-watter never killed 'em."

"And what killed them in the book, dear Ron?" asked Dot.

Bullock looked fretfully into the packet again and carefully re-sealed it. Adopting the most serious of furrowed expressions, he placed his elbows on the table and assumed his jutted chin and bulging eyes position.
"I'll tell thee what killed 'em. Nowt. In the book, nowt killed 'em. Still alive at 'end. And if there's one writer I admire as much as Conan Doyle, it's Orwell. Prophetic he was," he said gloomily, eyeing the GM seeds.

"Wyndham, not Orwell," corrected De'Ath.

"Tom, with great respect to your great knowledge, you will find that The Day of the Triffids was penned by George Orwell. I can tell you this, as I studied it for O-Level English Lit."

"Wyndham."

"Rubbish. Who's heard of Wyndham? Are you having me on, you devil? What else did he write?"

"'Midwich Cuckoos'. 'The Kraken Wakes'. The…"

"Alright, alright boys, you can settle this at home," intervened Bella. "I take it the seeds stay here?"

"Aye, with your agreement, Tom, they do. We can't risk Mr. Philp being ingested by a slavering giant pod."

"No indeed," replied De'Ath, nodding vigorously. "I would not want to be responsible for the genetic pollution of Oldside Allotment."

Bullock furtively dropped the seeds into a waste bin. He stretched and was eager to move on. "Well nice lunch, Tom and Dot, thank you, and the best bit to come. The Circu-Max cinema. Have you been to one of these things Dot?"
"I haven't Ron, how are they different to normal screens?"

"Oh, you haven't lived, Dot. The screen is so big that you think you are in the film! I went to one in Bradford about dolphins, by God, you felt like you were in t'pool with 'em!"

"Oh I remember that," said Bella lighting up, "quite dizzy I was!"

"Well, today's will be quite gentle, it is called 'Worm's Eye View, a Year on the Allotment'. Oh aye, I'm really looking forward to it. This will be the peace dee resistance, this will."

"Right, are we all ready?" asked De'Ath. "I will go and pay our bill."

After visits to the toilets, the party was raring to go, and followed the signs for The Circu-Max Cinema. "He-hey, not even a queue!" grinned Bullock, breaking into a skip. Bullock's good mood and enthusiasm infected the other three. But it was short-lived.

Bullock was glumly inspecting a hand-written sign hung on the handle of the cinema entrance. "What does it say, love?" asked Bella.

Bullock read the sign aloud. "Sorry. The Circu-Max is temporarily out of action. Engineers informed. Videos of Worm's Eye View' can be purchased in the shop for £9.99." Bullock looked most crestfallen. "Eeeeh, ah were right looking forward to that."

Bella patted his shoulders. "Come on, I'll buy you the video instead."

"Buy it. You must be joking Bella! We've paid thirty quid to get in and all we've had is a ride in a ghost train, a bottle of Infestos and some dangerous bean seeds. This is a money-back job, at least we should have a free video!"

Putting his case in the shop, he was given short thrift by the surly staff, and he demanded to see a manager. A man with a mournful moustachioed face appeared. "Good afternoon, and what seems to be the trouble, sir?"

"Well, I'll tell thee, er, Trevor." The man was wearing a name lapel badge. "We have not had value for money today. What we have seen is obviously sponsored to the hilt, and I wouldn't have minded, but for the Circu-Max being inoperable. I was very much looking forward to seeing 'Worms Eye View', y'see. Oh aye, and another thing. It says on the ads that the vegetable people wandering about are trained gardeners who can help you with your queries. But I suspect they are nothing but actors. Just people dressed up as vegetables."

"And you need to teach your coffee shop people some manners!" added Bella.

"And the Ladies are filthy," added Dot.

Trevor dutifully noted each comment in a pocket book. "And you, sir," he turned to De'Ath, "have you had a pleasant day?"

De'Ath looked thoughtful. "Well, I have got one problem."

"I am anxious to know," said Trevor, rather unctuously.

"Well," said De'Ath, "I did enjoy the antics of the tomatoes in the show, but, you see, they are fruit. And this is the Vegetable Experience. Not the Fruit and Vegetable Experience."

"Tomatoes not vegetables..." Trevor noted in his book, an eyebrow raised. "Now, folks, I am sorry you have been disappointed by the Circu-Max. How about four free tickets to come back another time. How about that?"

"I'd rather have a Worm's Eye View video," said Bullock petulantly, his lower lip protruding over his upper.

"No can do, I'm sorry sir," replied Trevor, extremely apologetically.

"We'll have the tickets then," said Bella. "Perhaps Surinda

would like to come with the kids."

Trevor disappeared and returned triumphantly waving four tickets. "With compliments!" he grinned.

"Oh well," muttered Bullock taking the tickets, "Come and have a look at this big Shed, ladies. But don't take any seeds from the slimy American."

After many rides in the GM train, Bella and Dot were ready to leave. Bullock and De'Ath sat smoking their pipes, watching the end of the second performance of 'Bounty of the Garden'. The white Lycra man began to approach them with a basket of Infestos, but he recognised them and ran the other way.

As the four trudged out through the portals of Vegetable World, they once again startled Reggie Radish, who had fallen into a light slumber in his patio chair. "Come again soon," he managed, hoarse and unconvincing as they passed him. He did not bother to get up. He sensed yet more dissatisfied customers.

"Mr. Radish, are tomatoes fruit or vegetables?" asked De'Ath rather brusquely.

"Oranges are not the only fruits sir, tomatoes be so too," answered Reggie theatrically.

"And why then, sir, are tomatoes performing in the "Vegetable Kingdom?" continued De'Ath sternly.

"Er, well, they are sort of honorary vegetables, aren't they.

I mean, you don't keep 'em in the fruit bowl, do you?"

"Actually, Reggie," said Bullock, with a glint in his eye, "I'm having a bit of trouble with me toms. Could you recommend me a nice cherry variety?"

Reggie thought hard. What had he been taught about tomatoes? "Come on, Reggie, you know this one," he thought to himself. He began to perspire. Bullock and De'Ath stared at him intently. "Moonraker!" he blurted.

"Moonraker?" spat Bullock contemptuously. "There's no such thing! You made it up!"

Reggie Radish had had enough. He took off his radish head and green feathery gloves, and laid them on the ground. He swept back the long grey-blonde fringe from his receding temples and stared at them coldly. "That is correct. I made it up. I am not a radish. I am not a gardener. I am a man. I am an actor. I actually hate gardening. And do you know what, you pompous right wing gay-bashing bully boys... I HATE BLOODY GARDENERS. Yes, that's right. I'll bet you've got an allotment, haven't you. And you spend all year there, and all you get is three bags of spuds, which you could have bought at Sainsburys for a tenner, and a row of mouldy carrots. Well you can bugger off. I'm not taking any more shit from the likes of you homophobes. I am off. I hope your garden gets bloody mildew. I HOPE YOU ALL GET MILDEW!!" At this the actor burst into tears, and waddled away in his radish bottoms, a sad and forlorn sight.

"RONNY!!" bellowed Bella, "what have you said to upset that poor man! Go and apologise immediately!"

But the cracked actor was already being comforted in the arms of Trevor, who was waving them away with a failed attempt at a cheery smile, which became instead a mournful leer.

Tom and Ron headed for the car, a little shame-faced. "Tell you what though, said Bullock quietly to De'Ath, "he'd 've made a bloody good onion."

They tried to resist their laughter, but could not, and quickly were hooting and wheezing. Bella had to bundle them in the car, herself beginning to cackle. After the sporadic explosions of fresh laughter from the front seats had died out, Bella attempted some conversation. "Well, I've enjoyed it, anyway. It's been a lovely day out. And just wait till Basker sees his squeaky parsnip man." Bella rooted the parsnip man from her handbag and gave it a good squeeze, but it made no sound. "What a swizz. It doesn't squeak!" she began to laugh again.

"Aye," sighed Bullock, taking a last look at Vegetable Experience as the sun began to cast an ominous shadow from the giant carrot, as he swung round the steering wheel, "what a bloody swizz."

Tilletson took another draft of Highland Park from his hip flask, as he watched the sun set on Basset Hill. But he tasted none of the heather-honey smokiness of the Orcadian single malt. This was how it had been for some time - since his interview with McMeddler, in fact. Nothing tasted good, nothing smelled good any more. Nothing was in colour, nothing was worth the effort. He had heard people talk of depression, maybe this was what he was suffering. But he had no interest in finding out. He had just had enough. If there was no room for his nursery in the world, then there was no room for him either. There was no more magic left in England.

It seemed the most natural thing in the world to do, end it all up here. And he knew he had the bravery to do it: put that familiar old barrel in his mouth, finger the silver locks, put his thumb on the trigger, say a quick prayer and, with an almighty bang, meet his maker. But the hard part was killing the dogs first. These old friends, getting on for seventy dog years each, would only pine away without him. His will, revised last week, had them buried with him and his land sold to anyone but Betta Gardens. Opening the rear of the car, he called the lurchers out, and they bounded, lithe despite their years, around the hill. He watched them in their athletic lope for the last time. He loaded two cartridges into the Greener.

"Fling! Frith! Heel now!" Immaculately obedient, the dogs ran to his side. "Sit down. Good dogs." He knelt down, holding their greying faces in his wonderful brown hands. "This is the end for us here now, my old friends. I'm taking you with me, and I hope you forgive me."

Tilletson stood up, feeling the age in his knees. He took a step back and raised the gun. Fling had no idea what was going on. Her small brain only processed the smell of a rabbit on the wind, which she would certainly chase if given the opportunity. But Frith, no great brain himself, did not like what was going on. He had noticed a change in his master lately and had been watching him. He did not like this trembling barrel aimed at his neck. With the instinct of the moment, he lauched himself at his master's chest. Man and dog fell backwards, and the sound of shotgun reverberated around the hillside.

Tilletson looked up at the charcoal sky. Frith and Fling were licking his face. He raised himself up on an elbow. "Good Lord," he said out loud. "Are those glow-worms over there?" Two greenish fluorescences ebbed from a tuft of grass nearby. He tried to get up to inspect them more closely, but his left leg did not obey. He looked down to see his boot exploded at the toe, and blood gushing from the hole.

"Oh bugger. Frither. Just look at what you made me do. I've shot meself in the foot!!" He laughed loudly and long for the first time that summer and rolled down the hill in joy, wrapped in a bundle of dogs.

- Chapter Four -

Autumn

It was mid-September. Though the days still felt like summer, the morning mist over the allotment was a chill autumn vale. The leaves on the trees were yet to fall, but the autumn hues were beginning to appear. In the allotment lane, millions of spider webs and threads hung festooned with tiny droplets of dew, sparkling in the white light of morning. On the plots, the growing season was nearly over, the energy of the summer sun locked up in seeds and tubers, for the leaves were fading fast, having done their work. And it was time to find those gardeners with the best bounty, with the greenest fingers. It was time for the annual produce show.

The 'Tredley Harvest', as it was called, was a particularly long-standing and prominent event on the village annual cycle. Indeed it was regarded by many locals as the highlight of the community calender. Perhaps one of the reasons for the above average interest in the local vegetable show was the intense competition for prizes and the legendary vendetta between Dredge and Philp. Philp and Dredge had been unfriendly rivals for the silverware for the last three decades.

In the Shed, De'Ath was closely inspecting the 'Tilletson's' calendar, which was hanging crookedly from a shelf. Tilletson was beaming benevolently whilst cradling a huge marrow, and beneath him the numbered squares were blank, save the 22nd, which was ringed heavily in red. "Just seven days to go, Ron."

"Aye, summer has flown."
"Damn shame about Tilletson's though. I can't believe he sold up to bloody Betta Gardens. Thought he had a bit more integrity than that. God knows where we'll do our shopping now."

"Aye, but it can't have been easy for him, Tom. Old rascals selling under the counter, undercut by national chains, difficult for these family businesses today. Poor bugger was on crutches when I saw him in town. Fell down the stairs apparently. Never rains but it pours, eh?"

"Yes, I am being too hard. I will drop in and wish him a good retirement."

Bullock was studying an A5 photocopied document entitled 'Rules of Entry for Tredley Harvest'. He was determined that he and De'Ath should mark their first season of gardening with a prize win, even of the most minor kind. De'Ath had protested that they should not expect even to enter the competition in their first year, but after lengthy discussions with his allotment partner he had conceded, as usual. But the question remained, which of the many categories should they enter?

"I just hope, Thomas, that our leeks have put on weight.

That chimney pot idea you had was a cracker, but it may have come too late. Still, we must stand a chance with our sweet peas, they are much better than Philp's, and nobody else around here seems to have grown beetroot."

"And our pumpkins are putting in a late rush, Thomas. The circumference of the largest was sixty-two inches yesterday."

"Pumpkins? Hmmm, mebbe, Watson. It would be a good one to win… the old boys are experts on the squashes. And they cheat of course. They say Dredge injects his with fluid."

"Well, let's go reccy and see what we can do. I'll bring the forms."

They bestrode their patch, which had an extremely eccentric look about it compared to the generally similar layouts of their neighbours. Along one length was a dying vine, the victim of early frost. Its grapes were hardly visible to their inspection. "Now Flowerdew was obviously talking bollocks when he said the Riesling grape could be cultivated this far north. This vine is Harry History. That's the last time I listen to TV pundits. I saw Titmarsh was appearing at BettaGardens the other week. What a laugh. Might as well have been Michael Barrymore for all the use he was. Should stick to novels. On second thoughts, mebbe not."

"Yes, Dot went for his autograph. Apparently he's a bit of a ladies' man."

"Well he's up his own smug bum if you ask me. Typical smug Yorkie. It was the saving of me to move south, Tom, to learn a bit of humility."

De'Ath looked up to see if Bullock was joking. Evidently, he was not.

"It doesn't look as though our late strawberries made it either, Ron," observed De'Ath of a brown patch of foliage.

"Just as well, mate. They would have accumulated toxic loads of those chemicals that maniac sold us. Couldn't have eaten 'em. Eh, but just look at the size of these blackberries over here, Thomas!" Over one side of the allotment, in the hedgerow, were big, fat wild blackberries. The bumper crop this year was due to the chemical decimation of the wild herbivores.

"'Blackberries, blackberries, nothing in the lane…'" De'Ath was very fond of quoting Sylvia Plath, but Bullock never seemed to pick up on it.

"Mmmm, sweet, too. What do you mean, nothing in the lane? Daresay we'll win a prize for these, lad."

"We can't enter those Ron! We didn't even grow 'em!"

Bullock was reluctant to accept this. "Well… we influenced their growth, Thomas, in a manner of speaking…"

"No, Ronny, absolutely not."

"We could make jam…"

"No!"

Bullock accepted defeat with a sigh. "Aye well, s'pose you're right. Ne'then, let's have a wee look at our muscle bound leeks." Along the centre of the garden was a cockeyed row of old clay chimney pots. Each was stuffed full of pig manure and from each poked leathery leaves. "Now then Thomas, let us marvel at the power of the chimbley. Let's see if we've grown champions in there."

"Are you sure, Ron? A week of growth to go, you know."

"Let's just 'ave a look at one, just to see, like. To see if they are worth entering, eh? How about this one in the middle." With extravagant care the pair lifted the chimney pot, disturbing the incumbent vegetable, and began removing the soil from it with archaeological precision. The leek was perfectly sound, but was rather average in size. Bullock chucked it in the bushes in disgust. "They can't all be like this. Try another, Thomas."

The next, the next after, and finally all the leeks, were harvested in a pile. During this glum harvest, Philp appeared.

Philp was rather impressed with the pile of leeks he inspected "Nice leeks, boys. They'll go a treat with the beef on Sunday, eh?"

Bullock was still unable to contain his disgust. "Beef be beggared, Mr. Philp. These were supposed to be specimens, not table veg!"

Philp eyed the vegetables with concern, his eyes narrowed. "Specimens y'say? Well yes, I see you grew them individually in chimney pots, fair enough. You fed n' watered regular?"

"Daily, Mr. Philp, at least," offered De'Ath.

"Mmmmm, what variety are these, then, Big Boy or Prizewinners?"

"Variety?" As he spoke, Bullock realised with a prickling heat on his neck that here lay the problem and what potential fools they might seem. He began his characteristic track-clearing. "Er, Prizewinners, I think. Probably a bad batch. Last time I use Simmond's seeds, I'll tell you. Ha ha!!"

But also as usual, De'Ath failed to notice either the problem or Bullock's desperate attempts at face-saving. "No, I don't think they were Prizewinners, Ron. Just a minute, the packet will be in the Shed somewhere..."

"Oh, don't bother yourself, Tom..." Bullock attempted to reign in his stablemate, but it was too late. "So, which do you use, Philp?" he asked resignedly, as De'Ath pottered innocently about.

"Big Boy. Just like me father and his before. Leeks have always been a strong point with us. Must be the Welsh in us."

De'Ath returned from the Shed, smiling foolishly behind his wispy beard and opaque round glasses. "Oh dear, oh dear, un faux pas." He handed over the empty seed packet to Philp. The leek variety, clearly marked, was 'Modesty'. Philp fells into thigh-slapping mirth. "Hoo, hoo, Modesty, oh, dear, boys, oh dear!"

Bullock joined him in wry mirth. "Oh dear, Thomas, I thought you would've noticed that you blind bugger. Last time you do the seed shopping. Oh well, we'll forget the leek challenge this year. What vegetable did Noah leave off the Ark?"

"Garlic?" offered De'Ath.

"Nope, leeks."

Philp, who hated puns with a passion, quickly recovered from his attack of laughter, and went about the rest of the plot, dour-faced. "It's a bit early for lifting your maincrop tatties, lads," called Philp, inspecting a pile of newly unearthed potatoes.

"Ah, well, that's deliberate that is," replied Bullock scurrying over. "I have been reliably informed that lifting 'em before the autumn rain comes reduces slug damage."

"Aye, but look at the skins. If you let the stems die, then leave 'em a couple of weeks to toughen in the earth, you don't get so much damage as you lift." Philp peered more closely at the pile of potatoes, and picked up one of the larger ones for a closer inspection.

"You look rather concerned, Mr. Philp?" said De'Ath.

"Do you mind if I cut one open, Death? You may have a problem here."

"'Old on a minute," protested Bullock. "That's a good tatter that, here, cut one of these tiddlers if you must."

Philp ignored him and, drawing a gardening knife from his pocket, neatly sliced the tuber he held in half. He peered at the potato again. "As I thought," said Philp with a pained grimace, "spraing."

"Spraing!" exclaimed Bullock, grabbing one half of the sliced tuber. "Spraing? Yer mekkin' it up, yer daft auld bugger. Spraing! I suppose me turnips have got boing, eh? What about the carrots, dengue fever?"

De'Ath chuckled, but Philp was not amused. "Just have a look, Bollock. It doesn't give me any pleasure at all, but look at this spud. Look at its flesh."

Both Bullock and De'Ath inspected the tuber, noting brown concentric rings in the white tuber flesh.

"Oh 'eck." Bullock's face assumed an aspect of pain. "Cut a few more open, Tom. They can't all be like this!" But they were. De'Ath and Bullock surveyed their potato famine with great sadness.

"You can eat 'em," said Philp, equally glum, "but I'm afraid they don't taste good."

"Spraing?" said Bullock, "That's not a variety is it? We haven't got that wrong like our leeks. These are Maris Pipers."

"No, no," replied Philp, "spraing is a virus. Can be poor watering, but usually it's poor seed. Where did you get your seed tatties?"

"Er, well, Bella found a bag of auld spuds under the sink going green and sprouty, so I thought I'd try them this year," said Bullock self righteously.

"Oh dear," said Philp taken aback. "I had no idea you were that desperate. You could have had a bag of mine."

"Yes, well, moving swiftly along," said Bullock, who felt in danger of being patronized, "come and see the rest of our plot. We must have done summat right! Let's 'ave a look at t'carrots."

Taking a spade, Bullock loosened a number of carrot plants and, taking hold of a handful of leaves, levered them upwards, shaking the soil from the orange roots as he did so. All three looked curiously at the unearthed specimens.

"How peculiar," remarked Philp.

"How strange," added De'Ath.

"'Ow bloody weird, you mean," spat Bullock, "what the 'eck's the matter wi'em?"

Philp took the gnarled, twisted vegetables and inspected

them. "Well, you get the odd funny one, but these are all twisted up into the oddest shapes," said Philp, full of curiosity. "I mean, you should have thinned these out, but even so. It looks like they are curling round each other for protection!"

"Look at this one, it looks like you, Ron," laughed De'Ath, unearthing more unearthly mis-shapen carrots, this one with a bulbous head and outstretched arms.

"Spooky, we've grown a mandrake crop!" said Bullock.

"Ooh, you want to watch out if you have Bullock," said Philp superstitiously, "shriek when you pull 'em up, mandrake. Witches' plant."

"Eh, yer silly 'olt codger, I'm kidding. Just mangled carrots. Eh, this one looks like you, Philp."

Philp had to admit that the carrot figure looked as though it was he, in a digging posture.

"Eh, let's search for one for Tommy, bearded carrot anyone?" said Bollock, beginning to dig. They removed the whole twisty crop, and had to settle for adorning a thin looking Siamese twin with some moss around its chin to complete the trio of voodoo dolls, which they set on the back of a wheelbarrow. They set down to regard their carrot images, De'Ath and Bullock lighting up their pipes.

"Mine looks a bit like a gonk, don't you think?" suggested Bullock.

"A what?" replied Philp.

"Oh, yes, gonks!" said De'Ath with a broad smile. "We used to call them troll dolls. I had a groovy troll with green hair. Used to like combing its hair. "

Philp and Bullock shot a sideways glance at De'Ath, who was grinning broadly and staring into the distance.

"Oh, yes, I remember now, we didn't call 'em gonks either. Ugly little buggers, those troll things were," said Philp.

"Gonks we called 'em. Gonks, maybe it were a Yorkshire thing."

"It suits you, anyway, that word, Bullock. Gonk. Do you know, we had a category in the Show years ago for the funniest vegetable? You lads would have swept the board. You could have had the mangled carrot army. I've never seen anything like this in sixty year of gardening." Philp shook his head solemnly.

"Aye, well, we wouldn't have been entering that category, thank you very much," puffed Bullock.

"It was quite good fun, until Dredge carved a bryony root into a little man throwing the 'Vs-up'. Caused offence, 'course, silly arse."

"Well, we'll keep our little familiars in the Shed," said De'Ath, picking up the vegetable men, "would you like to have yours, Mr. Philp, or will it keep our company?"

"No, I'll bloody have it," said Philp decisively and holding out his mitt. "I know you two, you'll be sticking pins in me!" He shoved the carrot creature into his pocket and walked off to the edge of the plot, by the hedge. "My word, you've grown some unusual stuff here boys. What's this?"

"That is one of the crops of the future, that is, Mr. Philp. Bamboo." said Bullock proudly.

"Bamboo? That's what the primitive tribes use to build their huts isn't it?"

"That's right, Mr. Philp. I have a primitive tribesman for a son-in-law; I'm growing him an ethnic lean-to. Us fellers, we still like it best in our mud huts, eh, Mr. Philp?" he said, gesturing in the direction of the Shed.

"Aye, there's something in that, Bollock. I've had me happiest times in my shed. More of a home to me than the house. Do you know," Philp announced with an air of pride, "I conceived one of my children in that shed?"

Bullock and De'Ath both wished they had not been told this, and De'Ath quickly changed the subject. "And you can eat bamboo shoots, too. Very good in stir-fry. Of course, pandas love the whole plant. No bamboo, no pandas."

Philp nervously scanned the undergrowth. "Pandas?! What are you buggers up to?" It would not have surprised him if a wild animal had been at large, after the events of the summer.

"And why have you covered your soil in tree bark? Too

lazy for the hoe, eh?"

Bullock leaned back, thumbs in waistcoat pockets. "That, Philp, is mulch. All us new gardeners use it. Suffocates the weeds, d' y' see? All different kinds of mulches. Everything from black plastic to rotting leaves."

"Aye the council use it on their beds. Looks bloody ghastly. Must cost a fortune. And what the bloody hell is this!?" Philp was inspecting a tall grassy plant crop. "If you two are growing drugs on parish land, your feet won't touch..."

De'Ath responded rather pompously. "I can assure you, Mr. Philp that there is no plant material of restricted use on this allotment. If you wish to..."

"Take it easy, old son," intervened Bullock. "I must say I'm impressed by your botanical knowledge, Mr. Philp. But this is not marijuana, weed, or waccy-baccy, as you suspect, but hemp, formerly grown for ropemaking. They reckon they will make paper out of this in years to come. I'm growing it for cloth, actually. My daughter in law, Surinda, reckons she can make a hat out of it for me."

"That's very interesting," Philp was genuinely interested. "It does look like cannabis though. My grandson showed me a plant. I don't disapprove actually. Don't want it grown here though. Could do without dealers and drug squad in the undergrowth."

"Not much chance of that. You'd have to smoke a field of this stuff. Doesn't appeal to me, anyway. If I took drugs, it'd be the hard stuff for me: morphine or cocaine. Now, if we could get some opium poppies...." Bullock began to muse, as he filled his pipe from his pocket wallet.

"Stick to the Sherlock Holmes books, Ron I can't see you as an opium addict," counselled De'Ath.

"Aye, now poppies, there's a thing you don't see much now," said Philp, "I see more of those big Icelandic buggers than you do proper field poppies. I conceived one of my children in a cornfield full of poppies. More poppies than corn there was then..."

Again, De'ath and Bullock did not wish to know of Philp's procreating habits. "A right bloody Lady Chatterley's Lover in your prime, eh Philp? Where was your third child conceived, Kew Gardens?"

"So you like our gardening experiments, do you Mr. Philp?" asked De'Ath, again changing the subject.

"Very interesting, indeed. You might want to enter your hemp plants in the show under 'Miscellaneous'. There's a cup you know. Won it once with some orchids I grew under glass."

"Don't fob us off, Philp. We'll have you with our pumpkins. Look at these," said Bullock with pride.

"Not bad for beginners," chuckled Philp, "but come and see mine." In Philp's allotment plot, all was colour and voluptuous ripeness. Pumpkins like beachballs nestled on straw mats.

Bullock pulled enviously on his pipe. "Miscellaneous it is

then. Eh, Philp, what do you get when you divide the circumference of a pumpkin by its radius?"

Philp did not trust Bullock. Was he inferring something untoward in his growing methods, or was this just another stupid pun? "I don't know, Bollock, what do you get?"

"Pumpkin pi."

Philp looked into Bullock's twinkling eyes. And he broke into a broad, toothless smile. "I like that one, Bollock. Pumpkin pi. That's a good 'un, that is."

The Tredley Reading Room always looked at its very best for the Annual Harvest Show. Donald Philp stood alone beneath the wooden eaves, already decorated with sheaves from the fields and old tools: a sickle, a pair of billhooks and a pitchfork. Studying the framed black and white pictures on the wall near the tea room, he noted that many had discoloured with age and damp. He was irritated that a photograph of a group of people taken outside the Hall had deteriorated especially badly. The ink from an italic hand still read 'Harvest Show, 1934' but most of the people had bleached to invisibility. That had been his first win, his chrysanthemums. His father was Show Master that year.

The door to the hall flew open, and a busy, portly woman trundled in, followed by several equally purposeful children. Philp removed his cloth cap. "Good morning to you, Mrs. Devellin. And young 'uns".

"Oooh, morning Donald. You are early today. Lots to do. Children, start getting the trestle tables out! It's going to be a hot day, I think". Mrs. Devellin already seemed hot and bothered, she usually was.

"Kevin, look sharp, get those table cloths out to air." She flung a bin bag at a dim-looking son.

Philp knew that was the end of the conversation, as she already became immersed in her apparently cheerless business. He walked into the morning air and the brilliant blue sky. It was late September, but Mrs. Devellin was right: it was going to be a hot day. Looking far up, swallows still preferred England's warmth to their African winter quarters. "Get later every year," he thought to himself, as he walked and squinted upwards.

Cliff Dredge wasn't looking either, as he arrived outside the Reading Room on his ancient Raleigh cycle. Or rather, he couldn't look, at least not forwards, as the wicker basket on his handlebars was filled with enormous turnips, with their foliage reaching to the heavens. Braking with his feet, he wobbled along and collided with the bird-watching Philp. Philp gave a yowl as he was rammed, Dredge's bike keeled over, and the turnips rolled into the gutter. Dredge extricated himself from the frame and looked up for the obstacle.

"PHILP!!!! You dozy old buzzard-pillock!! If those feckin' turnips are grazed, I'm gonna stick your scrawny neck in those stocks over yonder and pelt you with 'em. Sabotage that is. It's SABOTAGE, man!!"

"Don't you yell at me, you turnip yourself," countered a roused and winded Philp. "It doesn't matter if they're grazed or not, they're bloody half the size of mine!!" He swung out a boot and kicked one of the turnips down the lane. "There, it's bloody grazed now, mate. What you plan to do about that then, Microturnip?"

What Dredge planned to do about this clear act of escalation became obvious, as he approached a basket of tomatoes absorbing the morning sun to complete their perfect ripeness. He grabbed one in each fist and started towards Philp. "Well, Mr. Philp, these seem quite nice. Let's see how ripe they are, shall we? TAKE THIS!!!" Dredge swung around and threw the first, then the second fruit with all his might at the closed, freshly painted green door of the Reading Room. They slammed into the door, exploded into mush and dribbled sadly to the earth. "HAHA!!!" yelled a deranged Dredge, expecting physical combat with Philp to shortly ensue, and he grabbed a handful of tomatoes from the basket. "Come and get it Mr.... Ketchup!!!!!" But unexpectedly, Philp did not move. Slightly more warily, but still with full force, Dredge pelted three more tomatoes into the door. The door swung open.

"What the Dickens is going on out here....what...what...a mess!! Cliff, what on earth are you playing at?!"

Dredge was surprised to see Mrs. Devellin, and her army of children, who were also peering at the smashed fruit, and the clear culprit. "Oh, bloody hell, it's the Christian Mentalists...I mean, Mrs. Devilling and her do-gooding brood." He stuck a thumb out towards Philp. "Well, you see, he started it, he pushed me off me bike, kicked me turnips down the lane, and I thought well, tit for tat, like, fair's fair like, I'd, er, smash a few of his tommies, like." Dredge had calmed down enough to be realizing the childishness of his act. "Er, heat of battle like…?"

"What was that you called me, a mentalist?!!"

Mrs. Devellin, her husband and her family were devout Christians of the 'modern era '. They spent most of their time cleaning the church, organising play sessions at the Reading Room and generally being helpful and superficially 'good' around the village. They preached an informal, open hearted, modern bible scripture 'come along when you can and you can still come to Heaven' attitude in public. Along with a dozen or so like-minded old timers, they wore their dopey form of Christianity on their sleeves and on their window stickers. On closer inspection however, the Devellins were a narrow-minded, mean spirited, illiberal clique of gossips. In reality, they preferred no help from the other villagers, whom they tolerated through gritted teeth. It was *their* church, *their* village hall and *their* eternity.

Dredge hated the Devellins for their sanctimonious do-gooder smiles and called them the 'Christian Mentalists' to his mates in the pub. It wasn't that Dredge was irreligious; in fact he was rather devout, in an Old Testament way. He would have quite cheerfully attended church, but for the fact that he couldn't bear to watch another Devellin church brat numbly acting out the Sermon on the Mount whilst their mother played the tambourine.

But he hated them most for when he once tried out the Devellins' 'Christian' spirit. One Monday morning years ago, his cycle had a puncture, and he was eager to get to a farmers' market in the next village, a couple of miles way. Mr. Devellin was backing out of his drive in his Ford Mondeo. Dredge theatrically guided him out into the empty lane. "Ah, Archie, I wondered if you possibly could give me a lift. Me bike's bust, like."

"Where are you going, Cliff?"

"Just up to Curner."

"Curner?! Oh well, I could Cliff, but that's two miles out of my way... and I'm running a bit late... any other time, I'd be happy to, it's just this morning... "

Dredge had peered quizzically into Archie Devellin's smug, smiling, stupid, sweaty face and felt the Lord might forgive him if he hoiked a good green phlem from deep in his throat and spat it onto Devellin's 'The Lord is our Saviour' car sticker. He managed not to do this and, with all his restraint, was able to splutter, "no bother, Archie, no bother at all."

Archie roared off with an even broader grin, and after two minutes of a rousing self-rendition of 'There is a Green Hill Far Away', he forgot forever the favour asked of him. Thereafter, it became a bit of a joke among Dredge and his cronies to ask the Devellins for favours. "Oh, Mrs. Devellin, I'm a bit short this week. Couldn't lend us a tenner, could you?"

"Let's see, now, what's in me purse. Fifty pounds. Hmmm, sorry I need that. Any other time, though, just ask."

Dredge was awoken from his recollections by a shrill, angry voice.

"What was that you called me, a mentalist?!!" shrilled Mrs. Devellin again.

"Nonononono," burbled Dredge into the ground, replacing the tomatoes left in his hand into the basket. "I, I, … "

"He said he never meant it, Mrs. Devellin," offered Philp, as he began to pick up the remainder of Dredge's turnips,"the old fool just lost his temper, as usual. Didn't yer, Cliff?!!"

"Yes, well, that is, I niver, meant it miss, yes that is what I was saying, er… "

"Well, you can jolly well clear the mess up. Right away please." She strutted off like a puffed up turkey.

"You stupid old faggot, Philp. Right good start to the day you've made it. Still, I must say you kept your calm when I smashed yer marters. I thought I'd start World War III with that."

"Well, Cliff, you probably would have done. But for one thing."

"Yer yeller."

"Nope. Marters weren't mine."

Dredge squinted at Philp mistrustfully. He always was a good bluffer. "Well whose were they then?" he growled.

At that moment, Archie Devellin appeared with yet more offspring, carrying baskets of soft fruit and apples. "Now children, just put them over there to catch their very last rays of ripening sun, next to my tomatoes, oh, morning Cliff, morning Donald…"

Philp and Dredge tried desperately not to laugh as they scuttled off down the lane, but failed. They hooted and shrieked into the distance.

"I didn't think my fruit was that bad," mused the confused Christian, "perhaps I shouldn't enter it after all…"

By mid-morning, the Reading Room was a flurry of activity. A gardening army was gathering, arriving by foot, by bicycle, by tractor and by car. Attempts had been made to prevent parking directly outside the hall by the placement of cones, but as Ron Bullock's Rover towing a GettaTool trailer approached, De'Ath scuttled from the passenger door and like a busy spider, collected the cones like flies in a web.

"You can't park there, Ron, you are blocking the way!!!" shrieked a now hysterical Mrs. Devellin.

"We won't be a minute, love," bellowed Bullock, leaning over to the passenger window, "we've got some unusual stuff to unpack. Come on Tommyboy." Whilst others staggered under a huge cabbages or hauled over-laden trugs of onions, the disgorged contents of the Rover seemed mainly to consist of computer equipment. However, De'Ath furtively staggered in with large pots of tall vegetation, shrouded mysteriously in bubble-wrap. Finally, Bullock heaved in a bucket of cut flowers, sloshing water all over the floor.

Mrs Devellin appeared looking maniacal with a mop. "Don't bother yourself, Ron...I'LL CLEAR UP!!" she shouted, with a fake laugh.

"Oh, thanks very much, love, I made a bit of a mess there, eh?" replied Bullock without a trace of sarcasm. He began to inspect the wilted foliage occupying the bucket.

"Bugger it. These have bloody well wilted already. I thought we might be in with a chance of entering these in the 'mixed flower arrangement'.

"They seemed fine last night," offered De'Ath. "I put 'em in the big fridge just like we agreed."

"Well that's how they ship cut flowers, Tom, I've seen 'em arrive at the flower markets, refrigerated overnight."

Just then a huge bunch of chrysanthemums and dahlias walked in. Philp laid his perfect flowers down on a trestle table, the morning dew still on them, and began slicing stems with a Stanley knife. People came over to admire.

Bullock and De'ath looked up peevishly, each holding forlorn posies of floppy stocks. Philp's spirits were high as he worked. "Morning, lads, what have you there?"

"Oh, our flowers have gone a bit past their best, Mr. Philp, probably the heat of the hall," attempted De'Ath.

"But it's nice and cool in here," Philp replied. "Let's see… they were nice plants on the allotment these, people don't usually grow stocks. Oh dear, I see what you mean. Well, they look as though they've been hit by frost, but it's much too early for that."

Bullock had already realised that the fridge in De'Ath's utility room, cleared of its usual contents, had probably reached freezing point, and blasted the flowers, but he was ahead of De'Ath and had no time to intervene in De'Ath's response. "Well, they have been in the fridge overnight, but then, that's how flowers are shipped."

"In the fridge?" exclaimed Philp, "In the fridge? You don't cut show flowers till the morning of the show, lads! Oh, dear me. They were nice, they were."

"Oh, these aren't show flowers Mr. Philp," blurted Bullock. "We're not competing with these! These are just a little nosegay for our wives. On urn duty all day, keep a lady's spirits up, eh?"

"Quite right too. Just what I used to do for my Marie. Well, look I don't need all these, give them some of these instead." Like the expert florist he was, he began to trim and arrange several blooms. "So, what *have* you lads entered from your plot then. I've seen your sweet peas, very nice, but they're not winners, I'm afraid. Your beetroot looks nice, but I wouldn't want to be the judge who has to take a mouthful. I'm sure I can smell creosote on them. Mind you, Dredge's veg are all full of all kinds of toxic chemicals..."

On cue, Dredge entered with a theatrical swagger. "What's that, Philp, whingeing excuses for your maggot-ridden organic rubbish already?! Look at the state of your carrots, man, bloody stunted! Now *this* is a carrot, boy!" He brandished a carrot, fully two-feet long, menacingly in Philp's direction.

Philp glanced briefly at the object, continuing with his floristry. "Shove it up yer own arse; it's no good for eating." Dot and Bella entered with trays of tea for the exhibitors.

"There you are ladies, please accept these," said Philp, rather gallantly offering them both his arrangements.

"Oh, lovely," said Bella, "now Ron, why can't you grow flowers like this? Much better than that, ooops, I can't say yet can I?"

"Is this Mr. Philp, Tommy?" asked Dot.

De'Ath was still inspecting the wilted stocks. "Oh, yes. Sorry. Rude of me. Mr. Philp, my wife Dot and Bella Bullock."

"Well, we hear you have had some fun with our boys this year, Mr. Philp. Livened up the allotment I'll bet, eh?" said Bella with a laugh and a nudge of her elbow, which sent the old man off balance.

"Er, yes, in a manner of speaking, I suppose," replied Philp carefully.

"And who is this fine gentleman peering over your shoulder?" asked Dot. Cliff Dredge had evidently applied a large amount of Brylcream to the few strands of hair pasted onto his head and came forward deferentially to receive the cup of tea being offered to him.

"Cliff Dredge be name, ma'am."

Dot was thoroughly fascinated by him. Neither Dickens nor Hardy could have invented such an ugly little character. "Rich Tea, Mr. Dredge?" she managed.

"Don't mind if I do," he smiled, unselfconsciously.

Just then, Tilletson hobbled in, rather nobly, as if returning from a rather nasty war episode.

"Now who is that handsome man, Ronny?" enquired Bella.

"Oh, that's our mate Percy. Percy! Over here! Cup of tea for you!"

"Hello sir, how are you both, and are these your charming wives? Hello, Donald and hello, Cliff. How are you, Cliff?"

"I'm fine thanks for asking, Mr. Tilletson. No offence to you, ladies, but I'll take no tea with this stinkhorn." He trudged off, scowling.

"I'm really very sorry to hear you have sold the nursery and shop, Mr. Tilletson," offered De'Ath most heartfeltedly.

"Thank you so much, Tom, and for your loyal custom," Tilletson replied graciously, taking a sip of tea. "But the fact is, I cannot compete anymore. But it isn't the end of everything, is it? Just look at this lovely show. England does go on, doesn't it?"

Bullock presumed that Tilletson's rather sentimental speech was probably due to opiate medication for his injury. "Nasty fall, then Percy?" he said, eyeing his cast. "Oh, not really, Ron. Just lost a couple of toes. Really, a small price to pay for a lesson in life."

"Couple of toes?" exclaimed Bullock. "How the Devil do you lose a couple of toes falling down the stairs?"

"Aah, well, you see, suit of armour. Foot of the stairway. Crashed into it. Helmet falls off. Crushes toes. Freak accident."

Bella was most impressed by this handsome man and his glamorous accident. "A suit of armour at foot of stairs?"

"Yes, sixteenth century, Greenwich style. Rusty old heirloom, my dear. Anyhow, my dear Mr. Philp, are you expecting to win much this year, sir?"

"Could be me best ever year, Mr. Tilletson. I won eight firsts five years ago, going for ten this year. No one ever did that in this parish. It's been a good growing season, despite, er, various setbacks." His cup and saucer started to shake as he recalled 'Arnie Schwarzendigger'.

Bullock laughed heartily. "Aye, we've had a laugh this year old lad. I'll bet it was quiet before we arrived, eh, Philp!"

"Mmmm, it was, quiet..." said Philp, wistfully.

"Anyway, I am one of the judges this year. I must seek out my fellows. Lovely to meet you ladies." Tilletson hobbled away, under the admiring gaze of Dot and Bella.

"Will all exhibitors finish their preparations within the next fifteen minutes, then leave the hall..." announced a crackling tannoy system.

"Blinkin' 'eck, lets get busy on our miscellaneous, Thomas," said Bullock, wolfing down the rest of his tea. " We've taken your advice, Philp. Stand by for something highly unusual."

The next ten minutes were taken in elaborate preparations better suited to an international sales conference than a garden produce show. De'Ath and Bullock began to assemble a large display panel. The boards carried 'A History of Hemp' display, with rope, clothes, and paper items attached. Bullock pulled on an elasticated hemp cap, which being too small for his head, rode up the top of his pate and had to be pulled on again. "Oh, bloody hell, this cap is too tight, love!" Bullock complained to Bella. After manic attempts to assemble a PC, a mouse-driven interactive 'Questions and Answers -All About Hemp' was assembled. A ridiculous voice-prompt in Californian loudly invited the passer-by to 'toon into the five-fronded future'. They were ushered out of the marquee by a flustered Mrs. Devellin. "Time for refreshments," announced a sweaty Bullock. "To the beer tent, Robin."

"By Christ, I needed that, Thomas. Sweaty work these displays. The same again, old chap? What the hell is that you're wearing, man!?"

De'Ath had rather furtively removed his Fair Isle jumper and tied it round his waist, to reveal a 'fun' unbleached cotton t-shirt. Bullock leaned closer, and read the poem printed on De'Ath's chest. "*I dug, I levelled, I weeded, I seeded, I planted, I waited, I weeded, I pleaded, I mulched, I gulched, I watered, I waited, I fumbled, I grumbled, I poked, I hoped...so GROW......DAMMIT!*"

De'Ath smirked, looking rather pleased with himself, but Bullock was disgusted. "Oh, dear, put your sweater back on, Tommy, that's rubbish that is."

De'Ath looked crestfallen. "Steady on, Ron, Dot bought it for me especially for the Show. We thought it quite amusing."

"What, don't you like Tommy's new shirt, Ron?" enquired Dot, overhearing.

"Oh, no, Dot, er, it's grand, like," offered a contrite Bullock.

"Er, each to thee own, eh?"

"No need to pretend, now, I can see you don't like it," replied Dot with a smile. "But what is that hat, Ron? Are you joining the Rastafarian movement?" The hat was riding up the back of Bullock's skull again.

"You see, Dot," Bella explained, "he asked Surinda to weave him a hat from this hemp they've grown. She has a loom, you know. Well, she modelled it on a football, but of course, Ron has a head more like a beachball, so it doesn't fit. I rather like it though. Does it suit me?"

"Well," said Dot, "let me be careful what I say. You look like one of the originals on Coronation Street."

"Ooooh, Elsie Tanner?"

"Well, no," said Dot, beginning to laugh. "Ena Sharples."

"Ena Sharples?!" cackled Bella, "right, that 'at comes off right now!! Let's see what your Tommy looks like in it!" On tip-toes, Bella roughly pulled the hat onto De'Aths head, who smiled patiently, as the ladies gently poked fun.

"Just the half for me, Ron," he said.

"The half for the good doctor, two G & Ts and...PHILP!! I'M BUYING YOU A PINT!" Philp waved meekly in assent from across the tent, where he was chatting with some other ancients. Bullock threaded his way through the tables.

"There you are, old lad, now here's to the summer we've

shared and the silverware coming deservedly to you. Here's to Philp's Ten!"

"Philp's Ten!" It rang out in waves through the tent. Glasses were raised, "Philp's Ten", "Philp's Ten", "Philp's Ten!"

Just then the vicar of Tredley arrived at the tannoy microphone. An earnest young man with fluffy hair and owlish glasses, Daniel Easton was new to the parish, and nervous. He cleared his throat before making his crackly speech. Mrs. Devellin rushed to the front of the stage, hauling her brood, and smiled up at him unctuously. "Ladies and Gentlemen, welcome all to the Annual Harvest Show." There was a cheer and a round of applause. The vicar smiled nervously. "I believe it is a tradition to begin with a prayer and a hymn. So please, let us pray." All heads were bowed.

"You are the Maker of earth and sky
You are the Maker of Heaven on high
You are the Maker of oceans deep
You are the Maker of mountains steep
You are the Maker of sun and rain
You are the Maker of hill and plain
You are the Maker of such as me
Thank you Lord, eternally. Amen."

"What the bloody hell was that?" hissed Dredge to an old lag next to him, their gnarled hands wrung together, and heads deeply bowed. "What happened to a bit of fire, brimstone and penitence? Why old Reverend Foster, he used to make us 'umble before the Lord!" His friend nodded vigorously in agreement.

Mrs Devellin had now joined the vicar on stage, and fussily seated herself at the elderly piano. "And now, please, let's raise the roof, with 'We Plough the Fields and Scatter'," smiled Easton, thinly.

"Thank goodness that ain't been replaced by a pop song," said Dredge, clearing his throat. He liked this one. They all did. It had been sung at the Show since the beginning. The piano began its tinkling chords, and the whole throng burst violently into song.

"We plough the fields and scatter
The good seed on the land
But it is fed and watered
By God's almighty hand…"

It really was a rousing rally. The young vicar was quite overcome at the volume and fervour reaching him on the stage. When he had asked them to 'raise the roof' he had expected the usual scattered warble received at his Sunday congregation. This was what it was all about, he thought. A tear came to his eye and, raising his own tuneless voice, he punched the air in vague time to the crashing chords of the grimacing Mrs. Devellin. At the refrain, the volume grew even louder. The throng swayed in time, many swinging beer glasses as they sang,

"All good gifts around us
Are sent from heaven above;
Then thank the Lord,
O thank the Lord,
For all his love."

At the end there was a great cheer. The young vicar was almost speechless. "Thank you, thank you..." he managed weakly, before being led away by a concerned Mrs. Devellin for a cup of tea.

"Bloody poof!" spat Dredge, disappointed. "I thought there'd be a sermon about how we was all maggots in the face of the Lord. I used to enjoy that."

The gossip and chatter began to hum as the bitter began to flow. Everyone present began to debate whether Philp could achieve the magic ten. Rather like a general election, it was accepted that certain seats were safe: Dredge would win the carrots and cabbages, where Philp would win the cut flowers. This had been the case for as long as anyone could remember. The marginal constituencies would decide the Prime Minister of gardening and the size of his majority. The expert in these matters, a man called Swain, was no gardener himself, but a reliable pundit. He was explaining intricacies to a bunch of lags, with the aide of a home-made swingometer constructed from empty beer sleeves and jugs.

Philp himself was beginning to ramble pathetically about his lack of confidence in his outdoor tomatoes, and how he should have never used an Italian variety. Dredge was swilling beer frantically. He has been alarmed by the power of Philp's submission this year. There was no doubt in his head that the yellow rosette and Show Master accolade were to be Philp's yet again. He was resigned to that much. He also knew the majority would be large. Dredge had worn the rosette often enough to feel no envy for that. But no one had ever got ten firsts in show. The first to do so would be a legend. That this could conceivably be Philp made Cliff Dredge very, very anxious.

Back in the hall, the judges went skillfully about their business, awarding 1sts, 2nds and Commended stickers in their rightful places. They were taken aback by the hemp display, which seemed most dishevelled. One judge bravely attempted manipulation of the computer mouse, but only managed to exit the programme, eliciting an exit message of "Thank you for interacting". They moved on, baffled.

The marrow competition took longest to judge. Two perfect, huge specimens could not be separated for their shape, colour and variegation. They seemed identical in size, which was the main judging criterion for this vegetable, and a measure was made. With the tape in inches and tenths, no difference could be found, neither in length, nor in circumference. A discussion took place among the judges, and some scales were produced. One marrow weighed more than the other, and the result cards were duly laid.

Back in the tent, tempers were fraying. Dredge was becoming inebriated and hostile. "What's taking them so sodding long? Prob'ly poisoned 'emselves on Philp's foreign tomatoes. Should've grown English tomatoes, man!" he bellowed in Philp's ear, "ENGLISH!!"

Philp was by now quivering with nerves, jabbering madly about going down in gardening lore as Donald 'Ten' Philp.

Bullock decided the time was right for a joke. "Eh, listen to this one, lads. Two carrots were walking down the road when a huge lorry slams into one of them."

"Were they your deformed monster carrots?" cackled Philp.

"No, they were normal carrots. Anyway, an ambulance rushes the little fellow off to the hospital where he immediately goes into surgery. Finally the doctor emerges and approaches the other carrot, who had been anxiously awaiting news of his mate. "Tell me Doctor, how is he?" he says. The doctor replies, "I've got some good news and some bad news. The good news is he's going to live. The bad news is we're pretty sure he's going to be a vegetable for the rest of his life!" Heh-hay, a vegetable for the rest of his life!!" Perhaps due to Bullock's excellent comic timing, or perhaps due to the heavy consumption of ale, the beer tent rang loud with laughter. Both Dredge and Philp laughed a little too heartily, and one man had to be led away as his paroxysms turned into a dangerous cough. Bullock hooted, and De'Ath wheezed merrily. And for some preposterous reason, it entered De'Ath's head also to tell a joke to the throng.

"Ahem," he began. Heads turned to him quizzically. There was near silence. Some had never heard him speak before. Dot looked on with horror.

"Old King Cole was very fond of cabbage, " he began quietly.

"What's that he's saying...cabbage?" Dredge enquired, ill-temperedly.

"Yes, cabbage, Mr. Dredge" repeated De'Ath helpfully.

"I don't recall Old King Cole liking cabbage, Death?" complained Philp, "pipes and fiddlers, mebbe, but not cabbage?"

Bullock joined in. "Just shut up you old moaners and let Tommy here finish the joke. Goo on, lad."

With all eyes on him, De'Ath truly wished he had not begun. He opted for a rapid, blurted and botched punch-line delivery.

"Well, now, he sent out a decree that from then on whenever anyone ate cabbage it must be shredded and mixed with mayonnaise and bits of carrots. This is known as Cole's Law..."

The tent was as silent as a vacuum. Some looked on expectantly for the tale to continue. The smile on De'Ath's face was frozen. Dredge blew a raspberry. Swain booed. Philp frowned. "Cole's Law?" he muttered.

"Coleslaw, you old coot!!" exploded Bullock, "bloody good tale, that Tommy."

"Don't call me a coot, Bollock, I've more hair on my head than you bloody have!" And so the tension returned. Fortunately, at that moment the tinny tannoy announced that judgement was done, and the hall was about to be opened.

Usually, there would be only a gradual and polite flux into the hall to receive verdicts with fake nonchalance, apart from a few urchins who would run in to see if they had won the garden-on-a-plate competition. This year was different. The gardening army from the beer tent marched resolutely past the judges, the cakes and the pickling stands. They wanted only to know one thing: how many first prizes Philp had won. Dredge lurched madly up the aisles, carelessly colliding with a ten year old victoriously running back to show his mother his winning plate garden entry bearing a pink winner's ticket. The little garden exploded into dust as it hit he floor. Dredge croaked an oath at the lad as he staggered on.

Philp was behind the pack, with legs of jelly. De'Ath, seeing he was unsteady, took his arm. "Just take it steady, Mr. Philp. There's plenty of time."

As he was led into the hall, Philp seemed to enter a dream. The figures at the periphery of his vision, patting him on the shoulder, seemed to blur, and as he walked, he seemed to float. The room seemed quiet, and all was in slow motion. The music from 'Chariots of Fire' rang in his head. He gathered himself to walk alone through Tredley Reading Room on this decisive hour. He realised, in his trance, in a moment of revelation, that this would be his last annual show.

He strode confidently now, past the various tables. De'Ath would recall that the only sound in the hall then was Philp's boots on the wooden floor. As the ancient gardener approached the trestle tables, he began to count the pink first prize cards with his name on his magnificent flowers, fruit and vegetables. De'Ath watched the old man's hands clasped together at his back. The gnarled digits began to unfurl in sequence as he walked. 1, 2, 3, 4, 5, 6, 7, 8, 9...

"Nine" thought De'Ath. "One more and he's a local legend." His own heart began to beat loudly as he followed Philp up the hall.

Philp approached the marrow table, which was surrounded by the garden army. He saw two identical marrows, one with a blue card, another with the winning pink. He craned nearer, to read the name on the winning pink card, and his vision blurred again. De'ath watched Philp's hands, still held at the frayed back of his tweed jacket. Nine extended digits, one retracted thumb. The thumb began to straighten.

Philp was in a momentary delirium. He was receiving his first vegetable prize from Oldfield Gardening Society, a young man in a summer boater hat, his young wife beside him smiling radiantly beneath a bonnet woven with flowers he had grown for her. His old mate Snowy was patting him on the back. His brief reverie dissolved into a white mist, which cleared slowly, to reveal a pink card with a word in black ink. The name on the pink card before him read...'Dredge'.

Philp collapsed forward, like a man at the end of a marathon. But he did not fall, for he was caught in the arms of Cliff Dredge. The ancient adversaries stood locked in a bearhug, like two heavyweights at the end of fifteen rounds. Dredge's purple face over Philp's shoulder was etched in pained relief. Philp's face was bloodless, his eyes wrinkled tightly shut, his thumb retracted still. Philp whispered into Dredge's hairy ear. "You make it nine, then Cliff?"

Dredge patted Philp's boney shoulder tenderly. "Nine, Don. Marrow must have been ruddy close. Ruddy close..."

"I saw Marie, Cliff. She looked wonderful."

"She was the prettiest woman in lower Oldside, Don. Mebbe in all of Tredbury. C'mon, son, buy you a brandy. Ruddy close...ruddy close..."

They shifted off, arms around each others' shoulders. As they left the hall, they passed the tearful urchin and his mother, who was trying to re-assemble bits of the fallen gravel and lichen garden. Dredge paused and proffered a filthy fiver from deep in his pocket. "I'm a clumsy devil, young 'un. Buy yourself some seeds for next year. P'rhaps one day you'll be as good a gardener as this gentleman 'ere." The pair trooped on, exquisitely slowly, back in the direction of the beer tent.

Bullock and De'Ath were back in the hall staring at the marrows. "Well, I'll be beggared. Right up to the wire. Poor old Philp, denied his place in history".

De'Ath was inspecting Dredge's marrow. "Mind you, Ron, there's no contest in weight. There's no doubt."

Bullock was lighting up a pipe and, when he had succeeded, weighed the marrow in his own hands. "Aye well, that's never reet. Just as I suspected. Injected."

"Injected?"

"Sure as eggs is eggs, Watson. But to prove it... if he's been very stupid, he may have injected mercury. But I suspect merely water. A pint of clear water weighs a pound and a quarter. About the winning margin. Hard to prove, Watson.

No marks on the skin. It's an old trick, you ask any of 'em. Anyhow, let's go and see if we've tasted glory. Seems like our little exhibit is causing a bit of a stir."

Indeed it was. A group of young teenagers were playing expertly with the computer package, having rebooted it. They were greeted by Donut from GettaTool. "Is this cannabis? Did you grow it? Is that blow in your pipe, yeah?"

Bullock drew on his pipe, and gave an indulgent chuckle. "No, no, this is a relative of... hang on, what have you little buggers done to our exhibit...it's bloody been hacked at!!" The plant display had been reduced to rooty stumps and a few broken fronds. It had won no awards, the pink first prize 'Miscellaneous' card being placed next to a rather ordinary fuchsia.

De'Ath was shocked. "We've been got at, Tom. I know we've not been on the gardening scene for long, but well, this is just plain vindictiveness."

Bullock ruefully inspected the plants. "I suspect you are wrong Watson. I believe we have a drugs motive here, eh, boys and girls?"

"We never had your grass, mister. We knew it wasn't dope," answered Donut, disdainfully.

Bullock moved closer to the group, menacingly exhaling smoke. "Then perhaps you know who might have been mistaken?" After embarrassed and incoherent denials, the teenage gaggle shuffled off to the burger van.

One of the judges had noticed the fuss and came over. He was a military type in a blazer, with exceptionally polished silver buttons. "Yes, like that at judging. Sorry, chaps, had to judge it as seen. Jolly interesting idea. Saw a lot of it in India. Be those children I expect. Think it was waccy baccy. Teenage addicts. Bloody unruly. Better luck next year. Grow some beans next year, what, what!" The blazer turned and marched away. It suddenly halted and about-turned.

"Oh, don't bother with the hardware next year, there's good chaps. Not the Chelsea Flower Show, what, what? Cheerio."

Bullock and De'Ath had been transported back to their National Service. "Yes, cheerio, sir, thank you for the snotty advice," whispered Bullock under his breath. "Bloody brass. "Don't bother with the hardware". It was the hardware that won the bloody war, not chair legs like him. Still bloody ordering us about today."

Philp was beckoning them over from the beer tent. A huge yellow rosette, with 'Show Master' emblazoned in italics across it, was pinned to his lapel. "Mr. Philp. Well done, Show Master. Bad luck, too." De'Ath sat down next to Philp. "So near to the ten."

"Do you want me to autopsy his marrow, Philp?" said Bullock with a wink, pointing at Dredge, who was up at the bar.

"You'd prove nowt, Bullock. I know that Cliff is a cheat. It's a bent world, lad. In a bent world, I'll settle for nine."

"Wise words, sir, wise words... mediocrity, Mr. Philp, knows nothing higher than itself, but talent instantly recognises genius," announced Bullock pompously and rather irrelevantly.

"Well, I'm no genius, and you are certainly no talent!" cackled Philp. "Anyway, listen, despite all, I've enjoyed it with you fellers this year. Let bygones be. I've some information for you, Sherlock Bollocks. My grand daughter tells me if you want to find the plant hacker, try Spraggets Playground after dark." He winked like an ancient tortoise. "Go and give 'em a fright. Not enough of discipline these days."

Dredge wove his way between tables, slopping a tray of drinks all over the place. "Now then, Mr. Dredge," said Bullock, "congratulations on your narrow marrow victory. What variety was that now, Ben Johnson?"

"Ben Johnson? Now, I've never heard of that one, laddie. No, no, Big Boy, Bollock, Big Boy!"

"That's Bullock to you, Dredge, Mr. Bullock. An expert on intravenous administration." He mimicked a syringe being pushed, winking at Philp.

Dredge shook his gnarled fist, and delivered a torrent of old school abuse, interrupted suddenly by another public announcement. "And finally," fizzed the tiny tannoy," a new award, sponsored by Mr. Donald Philp, our Show Master. It is the Fred Snow Memorial Prize for the Best Allotment Newcomers. And this year, the award goes to… Messrs. De'Ath and Bullock!"

"Well, I'll go to the foot of our stairs," spluttered Bullock.

"Come on, Tommy, we've bloody well won something!!" Bullock received the tiny silver cup from Percy Tilletson on the small stage, kissed it, and hoisted it aloft, like the F.A. Cup, before passing it onto the stunned but beaming De'Ath. Bullock moved up to the microphone. "Ladies and...." But his words were lost in the throng. The barman Swain had wisely turned off the loudspeakers.

It was well after dark, and De'Ath and Bullock were lying in a ditch, fifty yards from a municipal playground, for the third consecutive night after the show. Their faces were blackened, and De'Ath peered through a pair of night-sight binoculars. Bullock was lying on his back, swathed in overcoats, ruefully contemplating the stars. "We'll give it half an hour, Watson, and then return tomorrow. We shall be revenged. By the way, why do potatoes make good detectives?"

"Because they keep their eyes peeled, Ron. You told me that one half an hour ago."

"Did I really? Did I ask you what the lettuce said to the celery?"

De'Ath replied with just a hint of uncharacteristic irritability. "Yeeeeees. Stop stalking me."

Bullock returned to star gazing.

"Just a minute," whispered De'Ath. "There's a couple arriving. I hope it's not that courting couple again. We could be had up as a pair of peeping Tom and Rons... no, it's a couple of lads... yes they are doing exactly what you said, Ron..."

Bullock lay unpeturbed. "Where are they situated, sir?"

"Hut at top of slide. Sitting down."

"Excellent. OK, Thomas, as planned. Check watches. Give me six minutes. Move in on the owl." He crawled off through the undergrowth, impressively silent. Six minutes later came the sound of a tawny owl, and De'Ath began his own commando crawl.

The two fifteen year olds were caught in their silent pincer movement, Bullock standing hands on hip at the foot of the slide and De'Ath at the foot of the ladder, as one lad passed a pathetically rolled joint to the other, in the glare of Bullock's torch. "I see you gentlemen take after ourselves, being partial to a smoke," said Bullock loudly.

"Are you fuzz?" said one of the boys in a surly tone.

"I like to think of myself as a detective, but we are not police. We are gardeners, actually," replied Bullock.

"Oh shit, Adam, it's them!"

"Shut up!"

"Oh, but it is we, Adam! Actually, we are rather glad you

didn't steal our computer as well."

"Don't know what you're on about..."

"Oh, you thought we'd leave all that kit without a security web cam did you? All taped laddy, faces the lot. Quite nifty steal actually, in and out before the judges. Oh no, faces addresses, names; your parents will be none too happy. Stealing and taking drugs, Adam. Oh, and supplying, too. That's the worse, er, rap as I believe they call it now."

There was no reply from the hut.

"Yes, you're in deep manure boys. Fortunately for you, you've crossed the right people. Even though you cost us a cup." added De'Ath.

"Y'see boys," said De'Ath in his bad American accent, "me and my pardner here is gardeners, and we have a lot of digging to do. And frankly, we don't much enjoy it. Now you boys look like you could handle a spade. Call it unofficial community service. Dig our plot, nobody need know. No police, no parents, no headmaster. How's that for a deal? Oh, and no more stealing and no more dope, or what you think is dope."

"Well boys, come down and think about it" said De'Ath, in schoolmasterly fashion.

The fifteen year olds seemed like very young boys as they finally came down the ladder. "We'll do it. OK?"

"You call this number tomorrow. Mr. Bullock. We'll fix up a time. Break parole and you're dead meat. Now get lost."

The boys sprinted away like hares.

"Excellent mission, Watson, and well worth the wait. I think we deserve a bowl before we return. Do you know, I haven't been on a swing in years."

Five minutes later, a young couple were about to enter the park when they were alarmed by two middle aged men smoking pipes, swinging gently backwards and forwards, their faces blackened, and wearing army fatigues covered in mud. The couple span on their heels and left in haste. The only sound was the rhythmic creaking of chains, the revenged men silhouetted against a rising harvest moon.

It was mid-October, and De'Ath and Dot were entertaining Bullock and Bella for lunch. The allotment had produced some new potatoes during the summer, which they had buried in a tin box in the plot until that morning, following a tip from Philp. Whilst the ladies washed up, the gentlemen reclined in front of the fire with immodest brandy balloons, extolling at length the virtues of their potato crop. Bullock, for the umpteenth time, was commenting on the quality of their vegetables. "By God, Thomas, those new tats were tasty. The satisfaction of growing your own good food, cooking it to perfection, and

eating it in good company; well, there's just nothing finer."

"I must say those lads made a good job of digging in that horse muck," commented De'Ath.

"Aye, we did 'em a good turn there. Do you know, one of them wants to help us out next year?"

The telephone rang in the hall. "For you, dear," said Dot, passing him the handset.

"Hello, George. Very well, yourself? Yes. No I haven't. Yes, that is my allotment. Yes. I can't credit that..."

Bullock realised at this point, from De'Ath's face and from the tone of the conversation, that all was not well, and he moved to the edge of his seat in concern. The conversation continued.

"Yes, I spend a great deal of time there. Oh, two dozen plots. Some not used of course. I can't credit that. No, of course not old chap. It was good of you to let me know like that. Yes of course. And to Margaret. Goodbye, George."

"Looks like you need another Remy, Thomas?"

De'Ath got up and began to pace the room, highly agitated. "You won't believe it, Ron. PIHSIL! are going to build a carpark on our allotment."

PIHSIL! (an acronym for Pile It High, Sell It Low!) was the second largest supermarket chain in the country, and a superstore was situated round the corner from the allotment. Bullock was, for once, lost for words. De'Ath was close to tears. Bullock sank back into his armchair. De'Ath continued to pace. "My friend George, on the council, got a tip off. They are applying for planning permission to begin work next year. Already greasing the right palms apparently."

Bullock was staring ahead. "We'll fight them on the beaches, Thomas."

"We haven't a prayer, Ron!! They built their store on a Site of Special Scientific Interest for Christ's sake! What chance do a few geriatric gardeners have against the might of supermarket progress? The parish council gets complaints as it is from local residents about how messy they think the allotments are. An eyesore, some say."
Bullock was beginning to think he was Winston Churchill. "We'll fight them on the landings."

"Most people round here moan about the lack of parking at PIHSIL! That allotment will be tarmac by July," wailed De'Ath.

But Bullock was airing the 'Victory' sign now. "Never, in the field of allotment gardening, will so much be won by so few. A pessimist sees the difficulty in every opportunity; an optimist sees the opportunity in every difficulty, Tom! We shall defend our allotment, whatever the cost may be, we shall fight on the beaches, we shall fight on the landing grounds, we shall fight in the fields and in the streets, we shall fight in the hills; we shall never surrender! Victory at all costs, victory in spite of all terror, victory however long and hard the road may be…" At this point, Bullock was so moved by his own words, he stood up and saluted.

De'Ath was too upset even to raise a half smile and slumped forlornly in a chair.

"Come on, old chap, where's the bulldog spirit? We shall fight those bastards for every grain of soil. The campaign starts here, Thomas."

Bella and Dot entered the room with laden tea trays.

"Tommy, whatever is the matter dear? Who was that on the telephone?"

"Ah, ladies," sighed Bullock. "Tea. Just what we need. We're all going to be busy in the next few weeks. And there's going to be a few changes. We'll be doing our shopping at FreshPrice instead of PIHSIL!. Tell 'em the tale Thomas. I'll pour the tea."

It was the first frosty morning, as autumn was giving way to winter. The Shed was being heated by a portable Calor stove. Bullock had just finished briefing Philp on the bad news. "So you see, Mr. Philp, that is the state of play."

"Well that's it, then. I was giving it up next year anyway. Shame, but what can you do?"

"I'm surprised at you, Philp. Lived through two World

Wars and rolling over for a bunch of German grocers. Oh no, I know you are made of sterner stuff than that. You, my fine man, are the jewel in the crown of my 'Artichokes not Asphalt' campaign. And you're not giving up next year. With our help, you cannot fail to do 'the ten' next time."

Philp sighed wearily into his mug, releasing a cloud of steam.

Bullock was unpacking a sales folder, containing maps, sketches, schedules, and timetables. "Gentlemen, this will require some proper planning. Now there used to be a conspiratorial snug in The Grasshopper, or rather whatever they call it now."

"The Pissed Newt it's called now," spat Philp. "Not been in for years."

"Yes, it is bad. But it is near. Coom on then, finish thee tea, and t'Newt it is."

The only pub within walking distance of the allotment was a tasteless refurbishment of a red brick Victorian establishment. A national restaurant chain had replaced the run-down bonhomie, ancient bar and good beer with bright kitsch, a full menu of awful food (or fayre, as it was decribed in the menu), and a children's sound-proof ball pit, which was the centrepiece of the pub. As the trio entered, two grubby-faced four-year-olds were engaged in a fearsome scrap, both screaming, but they could not be heard outside their hermetic capsule. Their paralytic parents fed pound coins at an alarming rate into a fantastically complicated fruit machine, with a control module like a flight deck. Nearby, an ancient couple were being attended by a twelve-year old waitress, who staggered under the weight of two huge plates of food. The steaks ordered were fully eighteen inches long and an inch and a half thick. The charred meat was buried beneath an avalance of oven chips and a deluge of battered mushrooms. But there was more to come: the waitress' piteously acned twin brother arrived carrying a truckle of revolting pallid vegetables.

Bullock knew every barman in Oldside, though he was a rare visitor to the Newt. "Now then, George, what new attractions have you added to the plastic palace since last I was here?"

"How do, Ron. Thirst got the better of your principles again, did it?"

"Aye. Usually does. Now then, er, three pints of Bitter Piss, please." The tap lager, Lager Piss, had not yet been delivered and a plastic sign, supplied by the brewers, had been attached to the handpump reading 'Piss Off...but don't go away, we're just changing the barrel...'

Bullock was watching the slavering pensioners, who were attempting without any success to dissect their steaks. "Good grief, George, I have heard of never mind the quality feel the width, but where the bloody 'eck do you get steaks like that to sell for £2.99? Never mind BSE, you'd die of exhaustion cutting it up!" Bullock cupped his hands to his mouth and bellowed at the male pensioner, whom he knew to be quite deaf. "NOW THEN ALF," he bellowed, mimicking a sawing action, "D'YOU WANT ME TO HELP

YOU CUT IT UP, OLD SON?!"

"Yes, very nice, Tom, very nice," replied Alf.

Alf's wife attempted a particularly robust downwards cut on her slab of meat; but her blunt knife skimmed laterally, scattering chips to the four corners of the pub. Neither ancient seemed much deterred and concentrated wordlessly and fully on the task of slicing and chewing.

"Looks bloody good to me," said Philp, smacking his lips.

"Oh, 'eck go on then. Eh, Georgio. Steak and chips three times. And don't bother with the pensioners' special. Pop down butchers and get us some meat off a cow, lad! We'll be in't snug."

After several pints, lunch, and an animated discussion, Bullock leaned back and pulled hard on his stone pipe. "Well, gentlemen. Those are the battle plans. We attack on all fronts. Legal. Political. Media. Environmental. Public campaigning. The lot. The works. Let's go to work."

Two weeks later, there was a knock on the Shed door. A reporter and photographer from the Oldfield Bugle were standing in a shower of rain when Bullock rose to open it.

"Mr. Bullock?"

"Press? Coom in, coom in lads. Out of the wet, come on in." De'Ath and Bullock had worked up a fug of tobacco smoke, and the photographer hacked a chesty cough. "Yes, sorry, it is a bit like an opium den in here, isn't it," aplogised De'Ath. "Let's leave the door open for a bit."

"Not many places to sit, I'm afraid," said Bullock, "well, apart from our thrones, obviously, but here, let's turn those pots over and you lads could sit on them."

"So, this is your, er, shed is it, Mr. Bullock. Very cosy. I'm Nick, by the way, and this is Dave."

"Nice to meet you both, this is Mr. De'Ath, my partner in gardening endeavour and, indeed, in our campaign to save this wonderful allotment."

"Yes, I interviewed Mr. Grigson from PIHSIL! yesterday. I gather they have offered to purchase some land for you on the other side of town. Much more suitable, he was saying, away from the railway, and so on?"

"What twaddle," snorted Bullock contemptuously. "Does he not realize that people have gardened this land for decades? Worked the soil. Improved it. Thomas here and I have invested in this soil. We have invested sweat, expense, and aye, even a little blood and a few tears. You can't just create a place like this. You wait till you meet our friend Donald Philp. Gardened man and boy here. Conceived children here, he did! Why, there's even ghosts of gardeners here! You tell 'em Tom."

Nick was already busy scribbling. Dave had become very interested in the way the light played in the smoke on these unusual faces and was beginning to take some arty snaps. De'Ath was rather taken aback that Bullock had mentioned his ghostly tale, as they had not discussed it further after Ron's prank. "Oh, er, yes, well, I don't think it is especially relevant to our campaign, but indeed, I believe I have seen a ghost of the architect of this edifice, in the very chair in which my friend Mr. Bullock now sits."

"A ghost?!" exclaimed the hack, who was getting more and more enthusiastic about this story. "Do you mean this Shed is haunted?"

"Well, I wouldn't...." but De'Ath was interrupted by Bullock.

"Aye, haunted. By a genial gardening spirit in an olt pulley."

"That's a fascinating angle for the story. Now, listen, Dave and I have to run, we have to cover a story in town. Some mad hairdresser is shaving all his body hair off for charity. Ouch, eh?!" The reporter and his lensman started to raise themselves from their flowerpots.

"Not so hasty, young fellow, you haven't finished here yet. That hairdresser berk can keep his hair on for a bit. I'm expecting some guests. And here come some now, bang on cue. You'll like this photo op, lad" winked Bullock at the photgrapher.

A host of gardeners began to appear, despite the light rain.

Or at least, people dressed as gardeners. Around forty friends and family, dressed in old sweaters, peculiar hats, Wellington boots and Barbour coats trooped dutifully down the allotment path, carrying trowels and seed trays. Ranatunga and Wendy pushed their small son along in a wheelbarrow. Bullock began to marshall his troops, handing out various tools and arranging the crowd for the camera, as if in a wedding photograph. He unfurled a huge 'Artichokes not Asphalt' banner, which was held aloft by the taller members of the throng. Various placards daubed with "PIHSIL! OFF" were distributed.

"OK Ranatunga, Philp aloft!" ordered Bullock. Philp tried to lose himself in the crowd, but was gently apprehended by the giant Fijian, who amiably hoisted Philp up onto his shoulders. "Now, here's your pitchfork, Mr. Philp", offered De'Ath. Philp was beginning to enter the mood of what was becoming quite an impressive show of local resistance and had something of the glint of battle in his eye.

"Not the fork Death, get me slasher, man!" De'Ath hurried into Philp's shed, where a row of cleaned and oiled implements hung each from their own hanger. De'Ath noted, as he removed the slasher from its rest, that the edge of the ancient hedging tool was as sharp as a Gurkha's knife.

The photograph arranged, Bullock took centre stage. "Right, on the count of three, everyone, ready, one, two, three..."

The group had been coached well; in unison they chanted "WE'RE GONNA FIGHT, FOR THE RIGHT, TO GAAAARR-DEN!" One of Philp's grandsons had made up the slogan, and Philp was particularly keen on it. He continued with a second solo effort.

"We're gonna fight, for the right, to garden," he croaked, brandishing his lethal slasher, prompting laughter all round.

"Well said, Mr. Philp," said Dot. "We'll show 'em."

"One more, now" said Dave the photographer, thoroughly enjoying himself, "let's have some real determination this time!" The gardening resistance tribe, with this new encourgement, began to look most severe and warlike. Philp looked especially menacing astride Ranantuga, who now sported a tribal war-mask. "Great picture, everyone!" shouted Dave, Nick was interviewing Philp, following Bullock's insistence. He was jabbering about Fred Snow.

"Now then, Nick," said Bullock, taking the reporter's arm. "Would you rather interview a hairless barber, or watch us declare war on PIHSIL!?"

Nick was opening his mobile phone. "Give me two seconds, Mr. Bullock. I'm coming with you."

"You stick around, kid," sad Bullock with a grin and locking the Shed. "You ain't seen nothin' yet." He blew loudly on an army whistle and barked his orders. "Right troops, we march on PIHSIL!!! For-waard, march!!!"

All the PIHSIL! stores had a uniform design. They looked like churches featuring a high tower, with a clock and weathervane, lots of stained glass, and built in a nave and transept style. Inside, the high pillars meshed at the high roof in a cheap pastiche of high Gothic. The 'Cathedrals of Consumerism', they were proudly called by their German founder. You could buy anything, from a turnip to a television at PIHSIL!, and you could buy it real cheap. When a PIHSIL! store opened, local traders within a radius of two miles just put down the shutters.

By the time of reaching the store entrance, the crowd had swelled to seventy. An acned youth in a security blazer three sizes too big approached Bullock. "Sorry, sir, you can't come any nearer the store."

Bullock did not even break his stride. "Get out of my way, you stupid boy."

The youth decided not to argue, and hared off to the managers's office. By the time a sweating and grumpy store manager had arrived, the protesters had occupied the whole main entrance to the store, linking arms and chanting. In the middle of the crowd, Bullock produced a megaphone.

"Ladies and gentlemen, we are sorry to have to disrupt your shopping, but it is very important that England takes a stand today. This German store is robbing us of our land. Our green land. The land where we grow crops for our children." At that moment, the local TV news crew arrived. Bullock was very happy to repeat his performance, as the cameras rolled. "We will not stand back and see our land destroyed to line German pockets." There were great cheers at this. This man..." he collared an embarrassed Philp, "...has farmed Oldside Allotment man and boy. He symbolises our campaign. We salute you, ancient gardener!!"

On cue the protesters broke into a song composed for the occasion by De'Ath, entitled 'The Ancient Gardens of England' to the tune of the 'Dambusters March'. Two men from the local brass band had turned up with a trumpet and a cornet; they had also brought a drum, which Bullock strapped over his shoulders and hammered gleefully. Bella bellowed the words stridently through the megaphone. Philp croaked a few words miserably, clearly hoping the ground would swallow him up. Dot was frantically leafleting alarmed shoppers with flyers marked 'Artichokes Not Asphalt'.

The police duly arrived, but did not intervene especially in preventing Tony from GettaTool in a tipper truck deposit a steaming load of horse manure in front of the protesters. A crate of live chickens was swiftly unloaded by De'Ath and Bullock, who set about releasing the squawking birds into the supermarket. Tony drove off speedily, relieved to have played his part and not to have been detained by the constabulary, who were still trying to assess what was going on. After a long conversation on her radio, a police sergeant produced a loud hailer from the boot of her car and addressed the throng. "Now then ladies and gentlemen, you have made your point today. Most impressively. Now move along please, and no arrests will be made."

There was a murmer, followed by one or two unconvincing

cries of "shame" or "arrest the bloody Germans," but the crowd meekly obeyed and started to drift off. Two lady protesters went off to start their shopping. Philp was particularly keen to be on his way.

"Not getting arrested at my age, Bollock," he muttered peevishly. "You do what you want. I'm off."

But it was too late for Philp to be off. Bullock whipped two pairs of handcuffs from his pocket and in an instant had cuffed Philp's wrist to his own. He ran inside the store, dragging the hapless ancient, who was mouthing like a goldfish. Using the second pair of cuffs, Bullock attached one end to a freezer leg and the other to his own ankle. He then sat down on the floor and began testing his megaphone, which was also chained to his arm.

"TESTING, TESTING. GOOD AFTERNOON LADIES AND GENTLEMEN... THIS IS A PEACEFUL OCCUPATION!"

Philp was forced to sit next to the ranting Tyke. He pulled his cap down over his eyes, in a forlorn bid to be unrecognized. Chaos was erupting in the store. Photographers and the TV crew ran in and began operating lights and flashes to film Bullock and Philp. Police were milling, chickens roaming. Shoppers were leaving their baskets and fleeing. Security men and every member of PIHSIL! staff were attempting to bring calm. A shelf packer in a PIHSIL! fleece shouted, "look, one of them's up there!!"

De'Ath, dressed in a hard hat and climbing boots had scaled one of the main pillars and, at astonishing speed, reached the beams thirty feet above. He unfurled and tied a banner reading 'Allotments not Asphalt', and sat triumphantly astride it. Dot and Bella applauded loudly. "Oh you can tell he were a climber Dot. Like a rat up a drainpipe he were."

"Hold on Tommy," sobbed Dot with pride and anxiety.

"Don't worry, love! It's a lovely view!" shouted De'Ath beaming, then removed a flask of hot water from a rucksack, and began to make a cup of tea.

"WELL DONE TOMMY MY LAD," megaphoned Bullock. "IT'S ALL GONE TO PLAN!"

De'Ath gave a modest thumbs-up, as he surveyed the confusion below. The press were flashing, interviewing and scribbling madly; and the police sergeant was becoming irritated at the turn of the events. A gangly constable approached Bullock, squatting down. "Now what have you gone and done, sir? Do you have the key to those cuffs?"

"Yes constable, I have it here."

"I'll help you out, shall I, sir, if you give it to me. A very impressive demonstration you've made today, if I might say."

"Yes, go on, alright son, now, where did I put it? Ah, yes here it is in me top pocket." Bullock shaped to hand the key over, but suddenly popped it his mouth and swallowed hard, his eyes bulging. "Oh bugger, constable. I seem to have gone and swallowed it." He winked at Philp, who watched aghast.

The police officer grimaced, stretched to his feet and produced his radio. "Parry 276. Yes, not too much trouble. We will need a set of cutters. And some ladders. No, it's not Greenpeace. Some rampaging gardeners, actually. Old enough to know better, too."

Bullock grinned at Philp, who had slumped shamefacedly. "Got em rattled, Mr. Philp."

"I knew you was trouble, Bollock, from the moment I set me eyes on you..."

The policewoman approached Mr. Philp, taking his arm gently. Bullock drew the megaphone and adjusted it to full volume.

"Do not harass this gentleman. Artichokes NOT Asphalt. Do not harass our peaceful protest. Allotments NOT Asphalt. England's green land NOT German superstore carparks. Get back woman, you are a public servant, DO NOT harass THIS ANCIENT GARDENER!!!! POLICE HARASSMENT!!!"

The policewoman waited until Bullock's tirade was over. "I was just wondering if you gentlemen would like a cup of tea. Your friend does look a little pale."

Philp was about to accept gratefully, but the rant continued.

"No PIHSIL! tea. CABBAGES NOT CAR PARKS!!!"

De'Ath began to join in, from the rafters, followed by Bella and Dot. Some of the shoppers joined in. "Artichokes NOT

Asphalt. CABBAGES NOT CAR PARKS! England not Germany!" Some of the PIHSIL! lads got excited by the anti-German sentiments and began to chime along. One lad started singing "Three Lions on a Shirt" and had to be silenced by the store manager.

It took about an hour for the police to remove Bullock, De'Ath and Philp with cutters and ladders. As they were led out to a waiting police car, a crowd of friends and family had returned to applaud. They came out beaming with clenched fists, giving 'Victory' signs to the cameras. Philp was shamed and hangdog. A group of PIHSIL! staff shovelled the muck into the rose beds and turned to watch the Oldside Three being escorted into the van by a smiling officer.

"End of Round One," shouted Bullock "Fourteen to go, ARTICHOKES NOT ASPHALT!!"

Bullock was trying to remain even tempered as he sat on the stairs with the telephone receiver clamped to his ear. "OK, my darling, I'm not raising my voice. I just want you to explain to me again why Mr. Titmarsh will not be at our event. We've got money, you know. Yes, I'm sure he is a very busy man. I'm sure he is. No we don't want Stefan Buczacki! No!! He's just not...box office! No, no, no, we want that smug, conceited, shamelessly self-promoting man of our times Alan flippin' Titmarsh!! Hello? Hello?!!"

"Hey, Ronny, come and see this!" called Bella, from the living room.

"Do we want Stefan Buczacki..." muttered Bullock, shuffling in from the hall in his tartan slippers. "Christ, it's Titmarsh!!" he exclaimed staring at the TV. The great gardener, author, and TV frontman was walking briskly into a PIHSIL! store, arms laden with fresh vegetables.

"Oh, Alan," sighed Bella, "What have you come to. Look, he's telling Sven Eriksson how fresh the veg is at PIHSIL! And look, isn't that Rolf Harris under that pile of oranges?"

"No bloody wonder he won't turn out for us on Allotment Day! He's sponsored by PIHSIL! What a bloody joker he is!"

"Never mind, love," said Bella, turning off the television. "Here's the post. It'll be alright on the night." She went into the kitchen to get Basker his breakfast.

"Kibbles and Bonio again," thought Basker. "One of these mornings, I would proper fancy a bowl of cereal like they have. The one with the tiger on it smells best."

"Bella!" shouted Tom from the living room. "Bella, come here, quick!" Bella shuffled into the lounge, as fast as her pink furry bedroom slippers would allow. Tom was scarlet over an opened letter, which he was waving about.

"Ronny, are you alright, love?"

"It's Briers!! He is bloody well coming! He will speak at

Allotment Day!" Bullock threw the letter in the air with delight, and danced to his feet. He took Bella's waist, and waltzed her round the room. "Da, dar, dar, da, dar, da..." he chimed. "Now, then Barbara, how did that Good Life tune go?"

The rain lashed down in torrents, causing lake-sized pools to collect around the allotment. The banners, so carefully stitched in red fabric on white sheets declaring "Save Our Allotment", hung in drenched and illegible folds. And the skies showed no sign of clearing. De'Ath's beard was plastered to his "Artichokes Not Asphalt" T-shirt, worn over several other layers, and Bella's Embassy was extinguished by the curtain of water falling from her umbrella, which had at least two broken spokes. "No bugger's gonna turn up in this," muttered an equally drenched Bullock, his flat cap dark with collected water. He eyed the trestle tables, containing trays of soaking vegetables grown on the allotment, all priced for sale. He was wrong.

Cliff Dredge came sploshing down the lane in his Wellington boots, guffawing at the tables. "Oh dear, dear, look at this lot of maggoty rubbish. Fifty pee for a bag of sprouts like those...you must be joking..."

"Bugger off, Dredge, " came a call from the Shed. It was Philp, with a mug of tomato soup, taking shelter.

"Don't worry mate, I won't be stopping long. And neither will you lot, so as I hear. They'll have you off here by Christmas, I shouldn't wonder."

"And what brings you with your fine sunny attitude, Mr. Dredge?" enquired Bullock.

"Well, I heard a rumour as Mr. Briers was coming, see. Don't suppose he'll be here in this. He is a Shakespearean actor now you know. Oh, he doesn't do sit-coms and ads now. He'll be after looking after his voice."

"Well that will be where you are wrong. Mr. Tilletson has just gone to pick him up from the station," announced De'Ath, waterily. "I must say, I thought his finest moment was narrating that rather surreal cartoon, Roobard and Custard."
"Roobarb?" sneered Dredge.

"Custard?" quizzed Philp, from the depths of the Shed.

"You remember, Bella?" asked Dredge hopefully. Everyone shook their heads.

"Roobarb and Custard," muttered Bullock, "I think you must have got mixed up, Tom. Briers never did anything like that."

"Doubting Thomas are we," he smiled his beautiful foolish smile, "we shall see."

"Don't go asking him daft questions, Tom, we've only got him for an hour."

Tilletson's Volvo arrived at the allotment gates. Richard Briers sprang out of the passenger door with a cheery wave. Tilletson stood gallantly above him with a multi-coloured umbrella. They all rushed excitedly to meet him. "My goodness, you have picked a day!" said Briers, with a spritely laugh, looking up at the rain.

Bullock opened the gate of the allotment with a great flourish. "Welcome to Oldside Allotment, Mr, Briers." Bullock seized the actor's hand and shook it with vigour enough to remove the familiar filed smile from the actor's face. "It really is an honour to have you here. Thank you so much." He was still shaking his hand.

"Really my pleasure, and who are these charming people," said Briers, in an attempt to regain his arm. "Now, hold on, I know you, I remember you from the news bulletins." Briers approached De'Ath, who was stunned into silence. An uncomfortable moment passed as Richard Briers stood with his hand extended, and De'Ath looked blankly back.

"Shake the man's hand, Thomas," hissed Bullock.

De'Ath finally shook hands. "Did you narrate Roobarb and Custard?"

Richard Briers removed his hand and felt like wiping it on his jacket. "That hand felt just like a fish," he thought. "Most certainly, I did," he replied. "Do you remember, derderderder, derderderder, derderderder, derderrrr!" Briers took De'Ath's elbow and to his own accompaniment, did a jig and a reel around the path. Everyone laughed.

Slightly dizzy from his reel, Briers wasn't quite ready for Cliff Dredge lurching up to him. "My God," he exclaimed taking a step back, "I mean, God afternoon, Mr. er, ..."

"Cliff. Mr. Briers. I wonder if you would do me the great honour of signing my autograph book. I am a great fan of yours and Mrs. Kendal." Dredge obsequiously proferred an aged and dog-eared little book.

"Of course, of course, a pleasure to do that, Cliff," said Briers, recovering his composure, but still captured by the mesmerising ugliness of Dredge. "Now then, I'll bet I'm going in with some famous names here. May I look?"

"Of course, of course," smiled Dredge, toothlessly.

"Oh, I say. Bobby Moore. Hughie Green. Dudley Moore. Ah, and Johnny Gielgud."

"That's right. All dead, now 'course. Seem to curse 'em I do. Sign me book and within a year, they pop off."

Briers, and the rest of the group, looked forlornly at Dredge. Briers signed the damp book resignedly next to the signature of Oliver Reed. "Now then, my petals, can't have you standing about in the rain," said Briers, quickly recovering his bonhomie, and taking the arms of Bella and Dot. "Now, what is it you want me to do precisely?"

"Well, the first thing we want you to do, Mr. Briers..." started Bella.

"Please, Richard."

"Well, the first thing we want you to do, Richard, is to have a nice mug of tea and a biscuit in our husband's Shed."

And so, Richard Briers sat opposite Donald Philp in the Shed, drinking tea and making the growing throng laugh as word went round he had come. Throughout the driving rain, he delivered a rousing speech of commendation for the allotment campaign, signed his name at the top of a petition and had his photograph taken for the local paper and with everyone present. He waved goodbye through the open window of Tilletson's car, clutching a soaking bag of shallots. "I do hope you win your campaign, Percy. I shall never shop at PIHSIL! again. What lovely people," he said, winding up the window, though his smile wilted slightly at the sight of the eagerly-waving Dredge. "Even the grim autograph reaper..."

The yellowing cutting from the front page of the Oldfield Bugle was pinned to the inside of The Shed door. The headline screamed "War for Oldfield Allotment", and the large photograph beneath was of Bullock bellowing down his megaphone, cuffed to a dejected-looking Philp. Another cutting from a pull-out story featured a ghostly, underlit portrait of De'Ath under a banner reading "The Ghostly Gardener of Oldside". And there were many cuttings and photographs with Richard Briers. One especial favourite, a Polaroid of Briers between Bullock, Philp, and De'Ath and signed "Best of British, Richard Briers" in felt pen, was propped up next to the pipe rack. Next to the cuttings and photographs were a series of eviction notices.

All was quiet and still, aside from the sleeping breathing of two figures curled on camp beds in sleeping bags and piles of blankets. Ron Bullock had been sleeping lightly these last four nights on guard duty, and a mistle thrush landing on the Shed roof was enough to wake him. He rubbed his eyes and smelled the Shed's musty, comforting smell. What they were doing was the right thing, he thought. With a great effort, he heaved himself to a sitting position. He looked down at De'Ath in the other bunk. De'Ath was lying perfectly straight on his back, his arms folded as if laid out in a coffin. He always slept like this and was always motionless and silent. "Strange bloke, De'Ath," thought Bullock, "but a good bloke. Good to be in the trenches with." He belched, stood up, scratched his buttocks and stepped out of the sleeping bag. He stepped into a pair of overalls, pulling them over the thermals and T-shirt he had slept in.

"Wakey wakey, Tom. Today is the day. Into the valley of death, son,"

De'Ath opened his eyes, at once fully alert. "Not quite six hundred to ride, eh, though, Ron! Now don't mock me now, but I dreamed of Mr. Snow last night. I'm sure he is here with us."

"Oh, aye, and I thought it was you tickling me toes!"

"I did ask that there was no mocking on this one, Mr. Bullock?"

"No, I'm sorry Thomas. We'll have to go and differ on this one. But I must say, your ghost story got a lot of media attention. That bit of telly on Sky News was seen in Australia, you know. Just think of that."

"And much good it's done us. Media. Petitions. Direct Action. Celebrities. Live-in occupation. And we've lost." De'Ath swung his legs over the bunk and sat glumly.

"Aye, but just think what a fright we have given them, Tom," encouraged Bullock, sitting down next to his ally. "Just think. We have scared 'em all the way to HQ. Fritz Poncenbacker himself, or whatever PIHSIL!'s founder's name is, doing TV here. And I'll tell you what, they are paying five times in mitigation what they offered. New nature reserve. Massive new allotment. New cycle route. No, lad , we've done alright. And your mate Snowy, he'll have a nice time haunting the frozen food section. Eh, can you imagine, you pick up a bag of peas, and buushh!! Up like Dracula he'll sit!!"

De'Ath picked up the kettle, chuckling, and shaking his head. He opened the door of The Shed. Fresh eviction orders pinned to the outside door fluttered like leaves.

As Bullock urinated into the hedge, causing steam in the cold November morning, he surveyed the battlefield. All of the allotment site had been bulldozed flat except for The Shed and its patch. Bulldozers and earth-movers lined the edge of the site, protected by sleeping Korean security men. About a dozen tents were pitched around the Shed, their occupants slowly waking to the dawn. Some were dreadlocked hippy types, others scruffy-looking students.

A particularly hardy young man, his bare arms covered in Celtic tattoos, was bivouacked in a trench. Filling the kettle at the standpipe, Bullock watched a naked female hippy performing a welcoming of the sunrise ritual. The Shed itself was barricaded in extraordinary fashion, with wires, ditches, and all manner of reinforcements. A sign with 'HQ' hung crookedly on the roof. Back in the warmth of the Shed, De'Ath turned on the morning news on the old Roberts radio.

"I must say, Watson, when I took up this gardening lark, I didn't expect to end up taking on the establishment using non-violent direct action supported by a bunch of naked hippies. This is the dawning of the age of asparagus, the age of asparagus, asparagus...ASPARAGUS!" Bullock burst into throaty song, as he brushed his teeth using a mug of water. "Eh, Tom. Botanists have developed a vegetable that eliminates the need to brush your teeth."

De'Ath concentrated hard. "Nope, go on."

"Bristle sprouts."

"Ah, got me, with that one you rotter," smiled De'Ath. "Mmmm. Make sure our action is non-violent, Ron. Remember what that sergeant told us last time."

"I must say it's against my better instincts. I'd rather take a few out before they get me. Come on, let's have a last game of chess."

The bunks cleared, they took to their armchairs and set up an old Waddington's chess set on an inverted flowerpot. For an hour they sat, silent, with camping mugs of tea, focused on their game and listening to the 'Today' programme on the radio.

At nine o'clock, it began to get noisy outside. There was a rap on the door. An excited student with no hair except sideburns and a long chin beard appeared. He liked to be called Ditch, to whom he referred in the third person. "Ditch says it's brewing, Mr. Bullock. A whole godamm army of security. The bastard bailiff. And they are firing up the earthmovers. Ditch is going to bloody have that bailiff." Tom and Ron peered out. A procession of bailiffs accompanied by police were indeed approaching the site. "No violence, Ditch. That's the rule. You just go and make it bloody difficult for them to move you, there's a good lad." De'Ath smiled broadly at him.

"Bless you both, and bless the Shed! May the spirits of the earth forgive them!" gushed Ditch, his eyes blazing. "Aye, well, nice to make your aquaintance too, lad," said Bullock, offering his hand. But Ditch was made of more passionate stuff, and he grabbed Bullock in a fierce embrace and then did the same to an embarrassed De'Ath. He then grabbed a handful of mud from outside the Shed and smeared streaks onto his cheeks and forehead.

"FRRRRRREEEEEDOMMMMMMM!!!" he yelled, as he saluted the Shed, span on his heels and ran headlong towards the advancing security men. He fell over in the mud well before he reached them and was hauled struggling by his feet into a police van.

Bullock roared with laughter, shut the door, and locked it. As De'Ath, as always, strangled Bullock into an inexorable checkmate, the sounds of battle raged outside. They peered outside, as wriggling bodies were lifted away and earthmovers moved ever closer. They both pulled on fresh 'Save The Allotment' T-shirts and baseball caps. They took a last look around the Shed. They shook hands.

"It's been a real pleasure, Ron. We really are losing a little bit of England here."

"Yes, I don't think that another allotment will be like this, Tom. Time for a new hobby. But it's been brilliant, bloody brilliant. One of my happiest times, though the ending is sad. OK, I'll be Butch, you be Sundance. Ready? One, two..."

Outside everyone else had been rounded up; the Shed was surrounded by security, bailiffs, workmen, bystanders well-wishers and press. There was a moment of stillness. A robin hopped onto the remaining bushes and sang. At the edge of the crowd, Philp was supported by his daughter. He looked very ill. A single tear rolled down his grizzled cheek, as he looked around at the devastation of his lifelong sanctuary.

Suddenly, the door of the Shed was flung open. The crowd cheered loudly. Bullock and De'Ath burst into the morning, Bullock with a banner reading 'THIS EARTH, THIS ENGLAND', De'Ath carrying a board with 'ARTICHOKES NOT ASPHALT'. Bullock knocked one security man clean over, De'Ath leapt athletically over him, and they entered the emotional embrace of their wives. The Shed was quickly sealed off by a ring of security men, and its contents removed. An earthmover was started and summoned in.

The crowd was silent. Philp covered his eyes, but he could still hear the splintering and crunching, as the Shed was removed from the landscape forever.

Thomas Bullock sat alone in his living room looking out at his garden. He knew that he should really go out and tidy the borders, before winter set in. The telephone rang. "Oldside 71928. Yes, speaking. I see. Oh, I am very sad. When?... I see. My very sincere condolences... Yes, we would like to. Wednesday. Fine. Twelve o'clock. Fine. Yes, see you then my dear. I was fond of him, too. Oh, yes,

Thomas too. Yes. Twelve o'clock. Goodbye."

Bullock lit a pipe and stood for a moment looking out onto the lawn. He sat down in his huge armchair and picked up the telephone. "It's Philp, Tom. He's gone. Yes. Yes. This Wednesday, the 23rd, midday. Oh yes, for sure. Good. Do you know, he told me that he would liked to have been cremated and his ashes scattered on the allotment. Yes. What a way for a gardener to go, eh? Anyway, they are doing the next best thing, burying him at Tredbury churchyard. Oh yes. OK, yes. Yes I'm alright. Are you OK, Tom? Yes, come round. OK, see you in a bit."

Bullock looked out onto his lawn, and he thought of the allotment. His eyes filled with hot tears, which ran in rivers down his ruddy cheeks.

It was the day before Christmas Eve, and it seemed an odd day for a funeral. As usual, there was no sign of a white Christmas or even of winter. Just a mild, short, grey day.

A throng stood around Donald Philp's grave. His many grandchildren and children circled the coffin as it was lowered. A lone piper played a lament, an eccentric component of the old man's will, since he had no Scots in him, his posthumous explanation being a "taste for the scirl of the pipes." Also in accordance with his last will and testament, in place of the usual wreath adorning the coffin, were great stalks of rhubarb from Philp's back garden, the sight of which relieved a little the tight, pallid faces of the bereaved. They supported each other as they let gently fall their handfuls of earth. Percy Tilletson, limping with a shepherd's stick, stood by Cliff Dredge, who sobbed quietly into his palm.

The priest said the last words, and the gravesiders began to dissipate, most to gather in the Reading Room, where life was mourned and life continued, with tea and egg and cress sandwiches. Only Tom and Ron remained. They removed their best coats and loosened their ties. With spades left to them by the old gardener and, as arranged with the gravediggers, they set to burying Donald Philp. The soil thudded onto the coffin and soon was piled above the grave in a mound. They cleaned their blades with an oily rag and, with arms about each other's shoulders, wished rest in earthly peace.

Summer

Philp's grave was a mass of beautiful wild flowers. Poppies, cornflowers and corn marigolds swayed their heads in the sultry southern breeze. A crafted hardwood bench seat, engraved with 'In Memory of Donald Philp, Show Master', was set next to his grave.

Ron Bullock and Thomas De'Ath arrived, wished Mr. Philp a good afternoon, performed some minor weeding, and then sat down on the bench, using the legs to knock out their pipes. They sat and smoked and chatted.

And listened to the grasshoppers buzz in the hot sun.